Acclaim for
Texas Two-Step

"Tough and taut, *Texas Two-Step* packs a punch. Michael Pool delivers."
—Sam Wiebe, award-winning author of *Cut You Down*

"Come for the gun-slinging, drug-dealing hijinks, but stay for the witty characterizations and whip-crack plotting that drives this humdinger to its action-packed denouement."
—Eryk Pruitt, author of *What We Reckon*

"Michael Pool's *Texas Two-Step* is a gritty adventure in the spirit of *True Romance* and *Savages*, filled with weed, bullets, double-crosses, and even a messy sort of redemption."
—Nick Kolakowski, author of *Slaughterhouse Blues*

"Michael Pool spins a story that's got kick, one that's got pace, terrific characters and some unexpected turns. Everything you want in a crime novel."
—Dietrich Kalteis, award-winning author of *Zero Avenue*

"Some things, once you get into them, they're hard as blue blazes to get out of. I would count Michael's book as one of them. It's almost impossible to put down, and, even when you finish it, it won't let go of you."
—Tim Bryant, author of the Dutch Curridge series

"Michael Pool's spot-on descriptions in this crime caper make for a good read with its own voice."
—Earl Javorsky, author of *Down Solo* and *Trust Me*

TEXAS TWO-STEP

ALSO BY MICHAEL POOL

New Alleys For Nothing Men: Crime Stories
Debt Crusher

As Editor and Contributor
Fast Women and Neon Lights: Eighties-Inspired Neon Noir

MICHAEL POOL

TEXAS

TWO-STEP

A TELLER COUNTY NOVEL

DOWN&OUT
BOOKS

Down & Out Books
3959 Van Dyke Rd, Ste. 265
Lutz, FL 33558
www.DownAndOutBooks.com

Cover design by Dyer Wilk

ISBN: 1-946502-56-1
ISBN-13: 978-1-946502-56-8

For my mom Kathy Mitchell
and stepdad George Mitchell,
your belief in me kept me going
when I forgot how to believe in myself.

CHAPTER ONE

"What the hell we gonna do with it now, Coop?" Davis asked. They were sitting around the basement trimming table in the biggest of Cooper's three Denver grow houses, the one he actually lived in when he wasn't crashing at his girlfriend Josie's high-rise condo in Lodo. Davis was trimming up a fist-sized cola and giving Cooper that same look he'd been giving him since they were kids back in Southeast Texas, the one that said "You got us in this mess, now how you gonna get us out?"

Cooper frowned, tried to shrug it off. This was gonna throw his entire life into something resembling chaos, but it could have been worse. If that Chicago drug taskforce had waited a week to kick down his boy Nelson's door, they'd have snagged Cooper's entire new crop of Bruce Banner with it.

Though now he needed to find a new place to sell thirty pounds of absolute head-stash Colorado dope, and pronto. Shit, somebody somewhere had to want it. Time to work the dwindling, all-but-dead network a little harder, maybe cut one of the other growers a flat fee to set up a one-time deal, though no one ever seemed to want to do it. He could figure out what to do with the next crop later. If there was a later. Things would work out because they always worked out. Cooper Daniels was just lucky like that, and he knew it.

"Coop?" Davis's annoyed tone brought Cooper back into the moment.

Cooper brushed his shaggy hair back out of his face and said, "Yeah, man, all right, no sweat. I'll make some calls. Could have been worse."

"I know it," Davis replied, "but that don't make it good, either. Even if you find someone to take it, who's gonna drive it?"

"We'll figure it out. Might have to get a little creative, is all. Everything will be fine, trust me."

"Don't think I don't know what you mean by 'figure it out.' How many more times do we need to end up in this position before you see the writing on the wall?"

"I'll let you know when I get there." Cooper went back to trimming, finished the bud in his hand and dropped it into the big red ice chest at his side, which was three quarters full. He'd been using the coolers to cure his crops for years, so long that the white interior was stained amber from the resin.

Davis stayed on him. "Dammit, take this serious. We ain't getting half the price per pound we could three years ago. Keep sending it farther and farther away, too. Network's getting smaller all the time. Seems like just about everyone we run with besides us has wised up and gone straight. We've had a good run, right? Saw more Panic than anyone I can think of, just about. Been up to our knees in good times since. Might be time to move on to something else, same as the rest."

Cooper stopped trimming again and looked up. "Lemme ask you something. You see me hitting the nine-to-five circuit? Some asshole in a suit telling me when to eat lunch like he's my daddy? This is what we moved up here to do, and we been doing it, right?"

"We were kids when we started. Weed's legal now.

Things change. I know Josie is ready to see you do something else, too."

"What's that supposed to mean?" Cooper asked.

"It don't have to mean anything. Blind fool could see how bad that girl wants you to clean up and put a ring on her finger, is all."

"Yeah? And then what? Quit going to shows, get me a job like Josie's up at Mile High Sports corporate? Set up a 401(k) and start shooting the shit around the water cooler on the cigarette break they don't even let you have? I'd piss off everyone in the building five minutes after I got hired. Besides, she's getting laid off in a couple months. They're going belly-up."

Davis sighed. "Have it your way," he said. "Ignore me and her and everyone else if that's what it takes to convince yourself. You know I'm with you either way. But we're gettin' the squeeze from every which one, and it's only gonna get worse. There's a retail shop on every corner selling eighths for twenty-five bucks. Same thing's gonna happen across the country, sooner or later. We can't exactly send it to China, so where's it gonna go?"

"I know one place it can still go," Cooper said.

Davis stuck his palms out in front of him. "Don't even say it," he said. "I told you I knew what you were thinking. That time we beat the rap down in Dumas we swore never again, and you know it. You don't fuck around with the universe like that."

"Might be we don't have a choice. Besides, we could send it through Kansas and Oklahoma, stay out of the litter box out there in the Texas Panhandle."

"Or we could get rolled up like a clump of shit in some other litter box. They have a gang-load of state troopers sitting at the Kansas border, pulling over anything with Colorado plates. And anyway, Nelson was coming out and paying cash, up front. We need someone who can do that, it ain't worth the risk driving it ourselves. Josie would flip out if you even tried. We don't even know anybody still in the game down in Texas anyway."

Cooper tossed another manicured bud into the cooler and said, "We still know one person."

Davis raised his eyebrows and said, "Tell me you're not thinking about calling Sancho."

"You really want me to, I'll tell you a bedtime story and kiss your teddy bear goodnight. But at the moment I can't think of anyone else to sell it to. And before you get all worked up about it, I haven't heard a word from Sancho in six months, so we might not even be that lucky."

"Probably got locked up somewhere with his daddy working overtime to beat the case. If hooking in with Sancho again is lucky, we must be on the other end of the rainbow."

"Maybe we are."

"I can't believe you'd even consider getting involved with that knucklehead again after what happened in Dumas." Davis slapped the table for effect, and a couple of untrimmed branches toppled onto the concrete floor. He bent down and picked them back up, gave one a smell, and put them back on the pile.

Cooper finished another sparse branch, cut the buds off it, dropped them in the cooler, and stacked the stem on a big pile laid out on trash bags on the floor next to the table.

He said, "All right, look, man. Half the crop's still hanging in the drying room anyway, so we've got a couple days to look for something else. Could probably sit on it for a month if I had to, but rent is coming due, and I about shot my load on that last stretch of shows. I'd need the money even if we did decide to shut down." Davis sighed again and said, "I guess just let me know what you come up with, and we'll get it done. Everything's cut down and packaged at my spot. Me and Sneaky Pete broke the whole setup down and tossed it in storage yesterday, so I'm officially shut for business after this. But, Coop?"

"Yeah?"

"I need you to tell me you'll at least work on something better than dealing with Sancho Watts."

"I'll do what I can, that's the best I can say."

Davis nodded. He pulled his latex gloves off and dropped them in the trash on his way to the sink, where he cleaned the scissor blades by dabbing olive oil on them and using a razor blade to scrape off the resin. Cooper thought about how they would have collected the resin as scissor-hash back in the day, when they'd first started growing, but they'd stopped doing that once the volume got so high that they had weed coming out of their ears. Davis said goodbye and walked upstairs and out the front door.

Cooper was sick of trimming for now, so he picked up the razor and cleaned his own scissor blades over the basement's industrial sink until he was satisfied they were clean enough to put away. He pulled off his own latex gloves on the way up the stairs, tossed them in the trash bin. He heard what must be Davis driving away as he crossed the kitchen. It was sunny, but he could already see clouds forming above the foothills to the west outside the window, meaning it would rain that afternoon.

With no cable and nothing else to do, it wasn't five minutes before he found himself swiping through his phone and stopping on Sancho's ranch house phone number. It had been six months since Sancho's last burner number went dead. He hadn't heard hide nor hair of Sancho since then, now that he thought about it. At the end of the day Cooper was running the show, and Davis knew it. Davis had always been content to follow his lead, so let him follow on this one. Cooper's green thumb had been paying his best friend's rent for almost a decade, and making him plenty of money to travel and party in the process. It was hard to deny that Sancho had a knack for getting into sketchy situations, but that didn't mean this deal had to have problems.

His penchant for outlandish behavior was how they'd come to give him the name Sancho in the first place. They'd been up at Sancho's Broken Arrow on East Colfax, seeing Netwerk: Electric or Signal Path, or maybe some other trance jam band he couldn't remember the name of anymore, when this wiry dude in patchwork pants and a T-shirt that said *Fuck Y'all, I'm From Texas* walked in the door. Soon as the guy laid eyes on Cooper and Davis and the other guys in their group, he'd walked straight up to them in such a way that Cooper assumed one of the other guys must know him. He stepped right up in the middle of the man stuck his hand out with at least a gram of white powder in his palm and said, "You boys want some of this here molly?" before taking a thick finger dip himself.

Though it turned out later that no one knew him, at that time Cooper had just shrugged and taken a few finger dips because, why not? And it was some of the best molly he'd ever eaten, as it turned out. Next thing he knew he was howling at the moon, eyes rolling so far back in his head he could about see what was behind him. And this stranger was right up in the middle of their crew, partying like he'd known them his whole life, whooping and hollering and dancing his ass off with his curly fro standing a foot above everyone else in the place.

When Cooper and Davis had gotten enough control of themselves to stumble over to the bar for another drink, Davis asked if Cooper remembered what the guy's name was.

"I don't know," Cooper said. "But he walks around this

place like he's Sancho himself."

That had made them both laugh so hard that the bartender wouldn't serve them anymore. Ever since then everyone had called him Sancho. Even down in Austin, where Sancho moved again after a brief stint in Denver, people called him that. Cooper figured that Sancho probably liked it a lot better than the name his parents had given him back in Wimberley, Texas: Elroy Watts Jr.

Cooper shook off the memory, not wanting to let his mind delve too far into what happened to them down in Dumas. It had almost sent him and Davis both to prison on a state jail felony, and Josie had never let him forget about it afterward. Instead, he clicked the button and dialed Sancho's number, was surprised when Sancho picked up after the second ring and said, "Talk to me," while someone hammered away on a djembe in the background.

CHAPTER TWO

Texas Ranger Russ Kirkpatrick was just pouring his second cup of coffee at his desk in the Austin DPS headquarters when he got a call from Javier Perez, the Travis County Sheriff's detective heading up the Weldon Robb investigation he'd been railroaded into taking on against his better judgment.

"Whadaya say, Javi?" he said as Perez's voice came through the line. "Was just about to catch up with y'all, actually. Senator Robb has been up my ass about this thing again lately."

"Yeah? Your ears must have been ringing. I've got something for you."

"About Watts? I thought he was out of the country still. Shoot."

"He's back. You might find it hard to believe, but something came over the wiretap last night."

"I thought that thing already expired?" Kirkpatrick took a sip of his coffee, burned his lip and had to blow on it.

"End of the month. Honestly, we haven't been giving it much attention anyway. I'll tell you this, Watts must have thought the tap expired, too."

"So our man's really back from Costa Rica or wherever he was hiding?"

"Oh, he's back. You better get over here and give a listen. I think we've got something that will stick to him, if you stay on top of it."

Kirkpatrick sat up straight. "Gotcha. I'll head on over in an hour or so. Anything else I need to know before then?"

"Not really. Just that I get the impression Watts thinks we've lost interest in him."

"What makes you say that?"

"Come on over and see for yourself. Play this one out right, I think Senator Robb might get some of that Texas justice he's always shooting off about."

"Sounds good," Kirkpatrick said, already flipping through his notebook to be sure he didn't have anything planned today. "I'll see y'all in an hour. Thanks, Javi."

Perez told him not to mention it and they hung up. Kirkpatrick took a few minutes to organize his desk and finish his coffee, then popped his head in the office to let his commanding officer know he'd be back later on.

He drove through La Mexicana and picked up an eight-pack of chorizo-bean-and-egg breakfast tacos on the way over. The Travis County Sheriff's Department hadn't been crazy about having Kirkpatrick forced into their world by a loudmouth state senator like Weldon Robb, especially with the warpath he was on. Even more so considering the grey line Robb had Kirkpatrick walking, thanks to a few favors he'd called in. Kirkpatrick always tried to ease the tension of dropping by with food or coffee. He knew for a fact there wasn't an officer within fifty miles who didn't appreciate homemade tortillas and the best damn chorizo sausage in the entire city, which was saying something.

He didn't blame them for not wanting him around anyway. Inter-agency politics had always been a problem, no matter where he worked. So had people in power, using their influence to get their own private sense of justice. Even back in the MPs, during the Gulf War, it had been that way. You just couldn't let someone come in and steal your thunder, at least not if you expected to have an upwardly mobile career trajectory.

But when a state senator's grandson twists off on psychedelic drugs and hangs himself from a Live Oak using jumper cables, some discomfort among agencies is to be expected. Without a killer to blame for his grandson's death, Senator Weldon Robb had jumped like a June bug on the idea of finding whoever manufactured the drug, so he could punish them instead. After throwing his weight around behind the scenes, he'd managed to finagle Kirkpatrick into a one-man task force whose entire life consisted of figuring out who had manufactured and sold the boy the drugs, so that the son of a bitch could be buried beneath the jailhouse.

Which had led Kirkpatrick by roundabout investigation to Elroy Watts. Sancho, as some people called him. Along with some help from Travis County, he'd dug about as deep into Sancho's life as anyone could expect. Travis County deputies had hemmed him up and taken his car apart three different times, to no benefit. Tapped his phone, staked out his farm from an adjacent hilltop. Kirkpatrick always felt that Travis County Sheriff's had come on too strong and spooked him, wasn't surprised in the least when Watts took off one day six months ago for South America. They didn't have much on him, but he wouldn't have known that. Probably he just felt the heat and his lawyer daddy told him to get out of town until things cooled off.

Now he apparently thought things had cooled enough to come back. If there was one thing Kirkpatrick knew about guys like Elroy Watts, it was that they never stayed out of the game for long.

Kirkpatrick pulled up to the Travis County Sheriff's office on Airport Boulevard and parked near the edge of the lot. He stepped out into the heat and put his beat-up beige Stetson on to shield his face from the scorching sunshine, then went inside. He flirted with Shirley, the dispatcher, for a minute, passed out a few tacos on his way back to Javi Perez's desk. Perez looked up from whatever paperwork he was messing with when he heard Kirkpatrick's boots coming down the hall.

"I can always tell it's you coming by the rhythm of your boot steps," Perez said as Kirkpatrick entered the office. "I see you brought a little something-something to ease the pain, too."

Kirkpatrick smiled and set the tacos on the edge of Perez's desk. "Figured a proud Mexican like you couldn't resist them," he said. He liked Perez, and they got along, despite all the departmental drama. The tacos were more of a bribe for the rest of the department to stay off his back, but he always kept a few for Perez anyway.

"Please, son. I'm as American as you or apple pie, minus that cheap cowboy getup. Third generation naturalized citizen."

"I know it," Kirkpatrick said. "'Cause you sound whiter than I do. Just giving you some grief."

"Well while you're giving, go ahead and pass me them tacos. And some verde sauce, yeah?"

Kirkpatrick nodded and passed a couple of tacos and a tiny plastic container of green salsa over to Perez. Perez wasted no time taking the first one down.

"So what've you got for me?" Kirkpatrick asked once Perez was wiping the corners of his mouth with a napkin. "I'm assuming he didn't just turn himself in and come clean?"

Perez smiled. "If only they all would, sure would make the job less stressful. I gotta tell you, though. We got lucky as hell on this. For a guy mixed up in as much shit as Watts is, he sure ain't practicing much caution anymore. Maybe he thinks he can't be touched, I don't know. But he put his foot in his mouth this time."

"Well then, let's stop beating around the bush and give a listen to what you've got." Kirkpatrick hooked a thumb in his belt loop next to his Ranger's star and leaned back in his chair, put a single boot up on the edge of the table. Perez looked at the boot but didn't say anything, figuring Kirkpatrick didn't mean anything by it, which he didn't.

"It's a Claim Two, but I already ran it up the flag pole to get it cleared. It still involves drug sales, so I don't think it will be a problem."

"Grayson isn't likely to shut much down with Senator Robb breathing down all our necks, so it should be fine. What is it?"

"Weed deal. High grade shit, and a bunch of it. Listen for yourself." Perez pressed play on the recorder and Kirkpatrick immediately recognized Elroy Watts's voice, but not the other.

"Sanch?" said the unfamiliar voice, which also carried a Texas accent.

"Well I'll be goddamned," Watts said. "Wussup, Coop?" Kirkpatrick scribbled that name down, still listening intently, trying not to miss anything over the banging sound in the background, some sort of drum maybe.

"Hell, not much, man. Where you been?"

"Been down in Costa Rica the last six months macking on shorty senoritas and getting some serious beach time."

"Six months, huh? That's a whole truckload of beach time."

"Yeah, I'm over it now. Anyhow, to what do I owe the pleasure? Y'all been seeing some shows while I been gone?"

"Some. We hit Oak Mountain and a couple others

earlier this summer, did most of the southern leg of the tour. Red Rocks last weekend was about the best damn run of shows I've seen in four or five years. Still recovering from it."

"I heard that, actually. What else is going on?"

"I...maybe I ought to call you back on your cell so we can speak freely? I don't have your new number, why I called the house."

"Haven't had one in a while. Just got back two days ago, been dealing with the jet lag, maybe a little culture shock. Costa Rica and Texas is about as opposite as two places can be."

"No doubt," Coop said. "I don't understand why you still live down there when the laws are easing up so much everywhere else."

"It's home. Besides, I don't see how cheaper prices are good for me."

"See there, I never wanted it to be home, got the hell out soon as I could."

"I get it. But why don't we get down to it, Coop. We can talk on this line just fine. I been dead to the world for six months, ain't nobody checking up on me."

"It can wait until later today if you want to go pick up a Cricket or something."

"No can do. I got a couple ladies stopping out for a little pool party, don't plan to step foot off the ranch today or tomorrow, if I can help it. Got an old buddy stopping up to play a little. Just got the pool back in working order, and I intend to make the most of it. I could call you back in a couple days when I make it into town though, if you're really worried about it?"

There was a long pause, as if this "Coop" were thinking it over, deciding whether to wait on whatever news he had. Kirkpatrick figured no way they'd keep talking after that,

13

was surprised when the voice said, "I guess we can talk around it now, and see what you think."

"Attaboy. Shoot."

"I don't know if you heard, but Nelson got rolled up in Chi Town a couple days ago."

"I didn't, but that's fucked up. What they get him with?"

"Enough is all I heard. Would've gotten him with a truckload more if they'd waited a few days, though."

"I see. So what's that got to do with me?"

"Well, they didn't get him with a truckload more. Which means I'm sitting here stuck with a truckload, nowhere to send it. Know what I mean?"

"I do. But again, how does it concern me? After Dumas you told me you were done with The Great State of Texas as far as business was concerned."

Kirkpatrick scribbled Dumas down and made a note to check the records up there.

"And I meant it." Coop continued, "But just now I'm in a bit of a financial bind, and it would surely help me to get this thing off my chest."

"What we talking?"

Kirkpatrick took his foot off the desk and leaned toward the recorder, thinking no way this kid spills the beans over the phone. The voice on the other end of the line hesitated, too, maybe sensing he wasn't alone on the line, but needing to get it out anyway. Finally he answered.

"Thirty elbows of Bruce Banner. Fantastic quality, too, one of the best crops I've done in a long time."

Sancho whistled. "Sounds a lot better than the schwiggity they had down in Costa. I might can help you out. Timing's pretty good, actually, with my boy coming up, think he's angling for some business. It won't be here in Austin, though."

"Why's that?"

"You kidding? Town's already full of Colorado's finest.

You boys got yourselves one hell of a saturated market up there."

"Tell me about it. All right then, where could you use it?"

"I think my boy is starting to do some work out in Teller. Why he's coming up tomorrow to catch up, or that's the impression I get. He didn't exactly say. I'll try to set something up with him when he gets here. Probably about sixteen a pop, I'm guessing. Will that work?"

"It'll have to, I guess. There was a time that was inconceivably bad, even if you came up here for it."

"Still wonder why I live down here?" Sancho said. "I'll hit you up once I get back out into the wild day after tomorrow. Let me see what I can put together."

"All right, do that."

"Good to hear from you, Coop."

"You too, Sanch. Try not to get so drunk that you drown in the pool, you hear?"

"Loud and clear," Sancho said.

Perez hit stop on the recorder. He and Kirkpatrick looked at each other.

"I see what you meant," Kirkpatrick said. "He was never careful, really, but that beats all. How does a guy like that make it this far without getting his ass locked up?"

"You know exactly how. Boy's daddy is a hell of a defense attorney."

"You mean *was*. I heard Pops might have run down to Costa Rica with him after they disbarred his ass over that mess down along the border. Luck must run in that family. I don't know how in the hell he avoided prosecution on money laundering and a whole host of other charges. Last I heard, they were still trying to make the case."

"Sure you do. The Good Ol' Boys' club wouldn't be so good if they didn't have some perks. Some folks think every county official up to the governor himself is corrupt around here." Perez grinned. "Probably some truth to it, too. No telling who that guy might have implicated if they'd let him burn. You snag this little shit now and maybe Daddy will come running out of the bushes and you can get him, too, make a whole new set of headaches for everyone involved."

Kirkpatrick frowned. "That your way of telling me I'm on my own on this?"

"You heard the tape. It doesn't sound like the dope is coming within two hundred miles of Travis County. That puts it out of our jurisdiction. I've done all I'm allowed by passing this on, and really more than I was told to do. A lot of folks around here don't seem to want to see this thing go any further." Perez looked around to be sure no one was within earshot. "If the department thought for two seconds this could bring even an inch of work back on us, you'd have never heard about this tape in the first place. The sheriff's had it up to his intestines with Weldon Robb."

"I figured as much. Thanks for the head's up, Javi. I'm assuming I can take the recording with me?"

"It's all yours my man," Perez said.

Kirkpatrick left the last two tacos sitting on Javi's desk and walked out of the building to his department-issued, four-door white Dodge Ram 1500, already dialing Senator Weldon Robb's personal cellphone number as he climbed inside.

CHAPTER THREE

Cooper went straight to the fridge and pulled out a cold 90 Schilling the moment he let himself into the tenth-floor, one-bedroom condo his girlfriend Josie's father bought for her after she graduated from CU Denver. She wouldn't be home from work for another half-hour or so, and while he normally didn't care to be in her condo alone, he was glad this time because it gave him a chance to think.

Davis wasn't going to be happy he'd already called Sancho, but he really didn't have much choice. Davis was already getting out of the game either way, and he needed his part of the money as badly as Cooper, even if he wouldn't say so.

By the time Josie walked in the door, Cooper still hadn't figured out what to say.

"Hey, good, you're already here," Josie said, setting down a paper grocery bag on the table next to his beer and giving him a kiss on the forehead.

"I am. You get off early or something? How'd you manage time to get to the store already?"

"I had a doctor's appointment this afternoon, so I just dropped by King Sooper's after."

Cooper studied her tanned, beautiful face, blue eyes looking more tired than usual. He could tell something was bothering her. "You feeling sick or something?" he asked.

"I do, actually. Been nauseous most of the week." She

sat down across from him and folded her hands together on the table.

"You want me to mix you a vodka soda?" Cooper asked. "Might settle your stomach."

"I don't think that will work."

"Why's that?" Cooper asked. She grabbed his hand as he reached to pick up his beer again. "Everything all right?" he added, something not feeling right.

"I'm just going to come out and say it, I guess," she said. "I'm pregnant, baby. Doctor says it's two months along already."

Coopers hair stood on end as blood rushed to the face he was trying to keep from registering any expression. They sat there like that for a moment, looking at each other, Cooper too afraid to take a swig off the beer, even though he really wanted one now, until she added, "Aren't you going to say something?"

"It's, ah, I'm just shocked, is all. Got some other really shocking news today, so I'm not totally on my game, as you can see."

"Okay, I guess." There it was, that look she got when she was trying to hide her annoyance, but failing.

"How...how did this happen? You been taking your pills, right?"

"I think you know exactly how it happened. And I have. They're not a hundred percent effective. Every now and again I miss one, it just happens. And I'd appreciate it if we didn't talk about it like I caught AIDS or something. We're going to have a baby, Cooper. At least I am."

She glared at him and he could tell she was close to crying. He realized what an asshole he was being.

"I'm sorry, I didn't mean it like that. This has just been one hell of a day," he said.

"Why? What else happened?"

"You're probably not gonna like it. Nelson got rolled up by Chicago PD. Guess they were on his tail for a while or something."

"Oh God," she said, a serious look now on her face. "Do...Did...Oh hell, do you think they're onto you and Davis, too?"

"I doubt it, otherwise they'd have waited a few days and snagged our package with him."

"I hadn't thought of that, good point. Still, isn't it possible they're onto you?"

"Anything's possible, but I wouldn't put a lot of stock in that. Local police departments don't tend to play well with each other, especially across state lines, so I think we're all right. Don't look at me like that, it's all good."

"I'm not looking at you like anything."

"Yeah, you are. You're looking at me like you're about to give me the 'time to grow up' speech again. Davis already gave it to me once today."

"That's because he cares about you, just like I do. Anyone can see the writing on the wall, Cooper. It's time to get out. Davis is. Besides, didn't you just hear me tell you we have a baby coming? Jesus Christ. I'm so naïve, I actually thought you might be excited." Josie stood up and tried to shove past him toward the bedroom.

"Whoa now, hold up," Cooper said, catching her with an arm around her waist and pulling her down into his lap. "I *am* excited. I was just shocked, is all. Got way too much on my mind and you caught me by surprise."

"Well, get used to it."

"I'll try. Have you thought about what you want to do?"

"I just found out an hour ago, Cooper. But if you're suggesting what I think you are, go ahead and stop right now. I'm keeping the baby. I'm twenty-nine years old, it was gonna have to happen sooner or later anyway."

"I don't know about *have to happen*, but I get what you're saying. I guess what I was really asking is, what's our next step?"

"I was hoping you might tell me that." She nuzzled his neck now to show him there were no hard feelings. Yet.

"Sounds to me like I need to offload this crop more than ever. Kids are expensive."

"They are. But where would you send it without Nelson? I'd gotten the impression he was the last connection you guys even knew anymore."

"Not the last one we know, just the last one we want to deal with. I've got something else in the works."

She pulled away from his neck and stared into his eyes. "Oh no, no way, Cooper. Don't even tell me you're talking about that fucking creep Sancho."

"I guess I won't if you don't want to hear it. Besides, Sancho's not a creep. He's a maniac, but he ain't creepy."

"A maniac who almost got you and Davis tossed in prison."

"Hell, Josie, that was as much on us as Sancho. I know the risks."

"Yeah? Well all I know is you said you'd never work with him again. You also promised me you'd never drive it out of state ever again. So..."

"So what?"

"So is Sancho coming up here to buy it?"

Cooper tried to lean away from her, which was futile. She was in his face and he could see she had no plans on getting up until he had some answers for her that made more sense. He sighed.

"I wish he was, baby. Guy like Sancho just don't need the money enough to take that kind of a risk."

"I see. But you do. Even with a child on the way." She shoved him away and stood up.

"Especially with a child on the way. I'm broke, pretty much. Rent's due on both houses soon, leases don't expire until December. I don't see how I have much choice. Look, you want me to get out of the game? That's fine. I'll do it. After talking with Davis this afternoon I can tell you my heart's not in it anymore anyway. But I don't have a choice on this. I already contacted Sancho, and he's on board."

"You talked to him over the phone about it? How'd you get his new number?"

"I called the house phone on the ranch his pops lets him live on out there."

"You called the house phone. I see. Mind if I ask you something kind of frank?"

"You're going to anyway, so shoot."

"Have you lost your fucking mind, Cooper? Does Davis know you called Sancho on a landline?"

"He knows I'm gonna call him at some point."

"But he doesn't know you already called him, caution be damned."

"No."

"Goddamnit, Cooper." Josie stood up, hugged her arms across her chest. "This is just peachy. I've had a hell of a day myself. I'm putting my foot down. No Sancho."

"I appreciate you looking out for me, sweetheart. But I'll be fine. Way I see it, we run this last load down there, drop it off and collect, then I come back here ready to become father of the year."

"Or you get rolled down there and leave me here to play single mom of a child with a convict father."

"That won't happen."

"How do you know? You're not psychic. The prisons are filled with people who didn't think it would happen to them, either. Let this one go, baby, to hell with the houses. They're gonna keep the deposits anyway, let them use 'em to cover the rent."

"I can't. I won't go out like that anyway. We've been at it for too damn long to just punk out. Besides, they'll put it on my credit, and that's no good either with a baby coming. We can use the money off this crop to start down another path. I'll pay off the rents and sell off all the equipment, and we'll have two legs to stand on starting out, at least."

"*If* you come back. If not, I guess I get to stand on my own leg."

"Sweetheart, be reasonable."

Josie bowed up at that. "I *am* being reasonable. You should take your own advice. Actually, you know what? Take a hike. I can't even look at you right now."

"You're kicking me out?"

"I'll call you tomorrow. Things have changed, Cooper. Why can't you see that? You're gonna be a father now, so take all this immature drug running bullshit home with you and when you come back tomorrow you'd best be ready to act like a grown man. Otherwise, I'm gone."

That spooked Cooper. "Gone?" he asked. "How can you say that? We've been together nine years. I love you."

"I don't see a ring on this finger, so I'm free to do what's best for me and my coming child, right? If that means moving in with my folks, that's exactly what I'm going to do. It's not like you've gotten rich doing this. You spent every damn dime of it out travelling the world, seeing Panic shows, living it up. That's *over* now, Coop. Don't come back until you understand that."

Josie tossed her hair back and stomped away into the bedroom, shutting the door behind her. Cooper sighed, would have mentioned that *they* spent all the money, together, but knew it would sound like he was blaming her. He finished off his 90 Schilling on the way out the door, his headspace more fucked up now than maybe ever before in his life.

CHAPTER FOUR

"Mr. Kirkpatrick, I hope you have some good news for me, 'cause I feel like a monkey fucking a football after spending all day at the capital," Weldon Robb said. "Where are we on our man Watts?"

"Solid timing on the return call, Senator Robb," Kirkpatrick replied. "Something just came over the wire today, that's why I called earlier."

Kirkpatrick was stuck in traffic on Mopac, as usual, easing along like all the other nine-to-five stiffs. His job was more like eight-till-you-go-to-sleep, but never mind that.

"Well come on then, out with it," Robb said. "I need something to bring my blood pressure down. Is the Watts boy back to making and selling that silly-syphon extract, or whatever the hell they call it?"

"Psilocybin extract. And not that I know of. It looks like he's getting back in the weed business, though. We got the idiot on tape setting up a delivery of thirty pounds."

"Y'all keep telling me how stupid the son of a bitch is, but you ain't caught him doing squat yet."

"That's about to change, I think. You hear this tape you'll know where I'm coming from."

Kirkpatrick nudged his way into the right lane and caught a dirty look in the rearview mirror from a woman driving a black Chevy Tahoe. He smiled back and gave her a wave, not sure if she noticed. He really didn't blame people who didn't like cops. Lately he wasn't much of a fan himself. He'd had enough of the job, considering the degree to which it had pulled his life apart these last two years.

Weldon Robb said, "Go ahead and send it over. When's all this supposed to go down, and where?"

"We're not all the way up to speed on the nuances yet. I'll send you a detailed report in a day or two, once I get it all ironed out. Problem is, I can tell you it sounds like it's going to go down in Teller County, and Travis County is shutting off the wiretap. They're sick of this case and everyone in it, I think."

"You mean y'all don't know where or when the dope'll show up and they're not even gonna try and find out?" Robb said, his tone sharpening more by the second.

"We know enough, all we really have to do is tail Watts and I'd bet he'll lead us right to the trouble I called because we need to put a tail on him and it sounds like Travis county isn't any likelier to okay that than my own chain of command. I need to iron out a few details and it would help to have some manpower."

"No count sorry excuses for law enforcement, every single one of you," Robb said, not even hiding the venom anymore. "Ought to just let him set up show right up in your department, way he's been handled."

"I don't know what else to say, Senator. I think you know we're really pushing the boundaries of what's ethical with this case. You know good and well why I'm a task force of one from a Ranger's perspective. Nobody wants to get caught overstepping."

"Mr. Kirkpatrick, are you suggesting I'm abusing my position seeking justice for my dead grandson? Ellroy Watts poisoned the boy's brain, I'll be goddamned if that son of a bitch gets to walk around free while he's buried in the cemetery, and I don't give a good goddamn what any of y'all think about it, I'm gonna have his ass before we're through. I'll have yours too if you don't get me there."

"I'm not suggesting anything, Senator. But we both know I'm risking my career on this, and it looks like I'm going to need some help to make the case shake out properly even if we can make it work." Kirkpatrick didn't mention that his career was already in the shitter anyway, didn't need to. It was why Weldon Robb had requested him in the first place, and they both knew it. "I think we need to get Detective Javi Perez from Travis county assigned onto the case as a special investigator to keep up appearances, make it look like we're just carrying on the work at their request due to jurisdictional restrictions. If I request a special detail for him, there'll be a hundred questions and ultimately I'll get the runaround, maybe the wrong higher ups will start wondering why we're making such a big deal about what amounts to a fairly small weed deal for Texas Rangers' resources," Kirkpatrick said. "You pull some strings in requesting him, there's generally a hundred 'yes, sirs, and I bet we can have him staking out Watts's ranch by late afternoon. We have him follow Watts down to Teller under my oversight, it looks like Travis County brought us in to overcome the jurisdictional limits of their case, plays better in court for everyone involved."

"Fair enough, I'll do it. But I'm warning you, Mr. Kirkpatrick. I'm running out of strings to pull, and you're running out of runway to get your career off the ground again. Act accordingly. I'll put in a call directly to the sheriff when we get off the phone. He won't like it but I've got a few sticks I can show him if the carrot won't work. And, Mr. Kirkpatrick?"

"Still me," Kirkpatrick replied.

"I want that chuckleheaded son of a bitch turning tricks down in Huntsville ASAP. Your future depends on it.

Understood?"

"Loud and clear."

"All right then, you know where to find me."

Weldon Robb hung up on him without saying goodbye, as was his custom. Kirkpatrick tossed his phone onto the bench seat beside him. Goddamn, he was sick of this fucking case.

The damn traffic in this town had been bad five years ago when he'd first been assigned to DPS headquarters as a special investigator. Now it was just plain unconscionable. Lately everything had felt that way, though, so maybe it was him.

If they managed to drop the hammer on Sancho Watts, Kirkpatrick would be headed south on the first plane he could catch for the Mayan Riviera, do some tarpon fishing down near Mahahual. But first things first, he needed to reel in the snake he already had on the line.

Fifteen minutes later he'd barely made it a mile down the freeway, but if it was any consolation he was at least starting to put together a decent plan on how to nail Watts to the wall by his balls.

When he finally made it to his apartment, he cracked open a Lone Star and sat down at the table to write out his thoughts on paper. Writing things down seemed to crystalize them in his mind. He'd gotten into the habit after reading about different types of learners in college, and discovering he was a visual learner. Now he wrote down every connection or detail he came across when working a case. He already had two full notebooks on Elroy Watts. With any luck the third would be the charm that finally put Watts down.

CHAPTER FIVE

Cooper left Josie's place and didn't even make it out of the building. He pulled up a stool in the bar area of a restaurant called Clark's that was housed in one of the commercial units on the ground floor of the building, a yuppied-out place he normally wouldn't have been caught dead in.

"What can I get you?" asked the bartender, who was decked out in some sort of old-timey bartending uniform below his thick beard and man bun.

"Something strong," Cooper replied.

"You look like a whiskey man. The house Manhattan is on happy hour right now, if that suits you?"

"It does. Put it on the rocks, though."

The bartender nodded and slid down the bar to make Cooper's drink. The idea that he was going to be a father had hit Cooper hard. The thought of Josie leaving him had hit him even harder. Possibly being a single father had hit him hardest of all. As overbearing as his own folks had been, he'd always been thankful that they were together. He knew Davis had always been a little jealous of it, having grown up with a drunk for a father and a single mother who worked 'round the clock to keep food on the table. The first time he'd met Davis, his soon-to-be best friend was riding a skateboard down the block in cowboy boots. There had been something he liked about him right away. Like Davis, Cooper had always had interests that a small

Texas town like Conroe couldn't satisfy. By the end of that first day they were best friends and did damn near everything together from then on. It had never stopped since. Davis had always seemed a little lost without a father around, and the thought of doing that to his own son made Cooper thirsty.

"There you go," the bartender said as he slid the drink in front of Cooper. Cooper dropped a twenty on the bar and the man brought back a five and two ones. Under different circumstances Cooper would have lost his shit at a thirteen-dollar drink, but now wasn't the time. His phone vibrating in his pocket took his mind off it anyway.

"'Sup man?" he said to Davis when he answered.

"You had some time to get your head straight?" Davis asked.

"Not exactly. In fact, my head feels like it's filled with Jell-O at the moment. Josie just told me she's pregnant."

"Well shit, Cooper, that's great," Davis said, not even a second of hesitation.

"Is it? I ain't so sure just now, things being like they are."

"It was bound to happen, man. Y'all been together long enough. Just another sign it's time to move on, wouldn't you say?"

"See that's just it, bud. It's making her question whether I'm the right man for the job."

"On account of what?"

"On account of I made a phone call this afternoon that ain't likely to make you any happier than it made her."

The line went quiet for a moment. "You didn't, did you?"

"Best if we discuss this in person.

"I get it. Where you at?"

"I'm in that chach bar downstairs from Josie's condo, but I ain't staying." The bartender gave him a sour look for the insult, but Cooper ignored it.

Davis whistled. "Damn, Coop, you must be hard up then."

"Thirteen-dollar drinks and everything, brother."

"Let's meet back over at the main house and talk this through, sound good?"

"Give me twenty and I'll be there." Cooper hung up and drained his entire cocktail, picked up the five-dollar bill and rolled out the front door.

Davis's truck was parked in front of the house when Cooper pulled into the driveway. Davis had a grin on his face when they met at the front door.

"Bring it on in here," Davis said, pulling him in for a hug. "Whether you're ready to understand it or not, I'm happy for you, Coop. If I had a girl like Josie I might have to get one brewing myself. Remember we used to imagine ourselves raising a couple boys up side by side? Coaching pee wee football, teachin' 'em how to shoot and hunt like your dad showed us?"

"I do. But who says it will be a boy anyway?" Cooper unlocked the door and they stepped inside.

"Pull up a chair and sit with me for a minute, man," Davis said, gesturing toward the small kitchen table that was shoved up against the yellowed wall. "I've got something I want to say to you before we talk shop."

Cooper had a good idea what was coming. Davis had always been the sentimental one between them. "All right, come on out with it," Cooper said.

"I want you to know that you and Josie are like family to me. Y'all are two of the most important people in my life, and I hope you'll do right by this thing. I love you, man, my whole life you been there for me whenever I needed you, and I intend to be there for you now. I know you done called Sancho, and I don't agree, but if you think it's what we got to do to get through this, I'm gonna do it with you. But only if it means you get out afterwards and focus on this kid, you got me?"

Cooper stood up and grabbed them a couple of beers from the fridge, still uncomfortable after all these years with the heavy sentimentality Davis sometimes displayed. He loved his friend too, he just hated to say stuff like that out loud, had always hated it. It made him realize he was like his father more than he cared to admit.

"I get it. But if we go through with this thing, I'm not sure Josie is gonna have me back around either way. She wants me to forget about the crop and move on."

"She'll cool off. She always does. You have to admit you're kind of a pain in the ass." Davis smiled, trying to lighten the mood.

Cooper grinned a little, too. "Okay enough of all that mess. You're right. But we got to make some plans."

"You just tell me when we leave for Austin and I'm there."

"See, that's just it. We ain't going to Austin."

"But you did call Sancho, right?"

"Yep. Thing is, he ain't got use for it in A-town. Sounds like we're headed out to Teller."

The air seemed to suck out of the room just a bit at that. Cooper had had a feeling that might sober Davis up a bit, and he'd been right.

"Shit," Davis said. "I should have known it would be something like that. Got any idea who we'll be dealing with down there?"

"I don't. And I'm not feeling all that great about it either. Place is conservative creepy as hell. It's a heck of a risk, but I don't see any other way."

"I understand that," Davis said, taking a long pull on

his beer. "Got any ideas on how we can minimize the risk?"

"Not just now. You?"

"Nope."

"I suppose we have a few days to give it some thought. I'll see what Sancho has to say after that. He's supposed to call me. In the meantime, I was hoping you might see about wholesaling off all the grow equipment before we leave. I figure if I at least leave Josie with a stack of cash and a decisive act toward moving on she'll feel a little better about the whole thing."

"I might could swing that. Let me give Small Paul a call and see if he's still dealing used equipment."

"Good idea. I'll make sure everything gets weighed and packaged up, and see what I can do about finding us a driver in the meantime."

"You want me to go ahead and grab some cases of butane and set it up with Miles to blow all the trim into earwax?" Davis asked.

"Yeah, that's probably a good idea, too. Like I said, the more money I leave Josie with, the better. Glad there's still one product that can be sold around here." Cooper finished his beer, went to the fridge and got out another.

"We could just blow the whole crop into wax, sell that?" Davis said.

"You know how it is. Buds never seem to make as much hash as the trim, and we'd be getting pennies on the dollar by the time we were through buying that much butane, not to mention the risk of blowing a square block of the city off the map." Cooper drained his beer.

"You planning on tying one on, or what?" Davis asked.

"Managing the stress. Why, you feel like getting out on the town?"

"I heard Jerry Joseph might be sitting in with The Hairbenders over at Cervante's tonight."

"I'm into it if you are," Cooper said, grabbing another beer from the fridge. "Terry's girl is working the bar up there now, probably hook up a few drinks."

Davis finished his beer, too, took both their empties and rinsed them out, then dropped them in the recycle bin. "I'll tell you what; let me head home and grab a shower and some better clothes first. Meet you here around nine?"

"That'll hunt," Cooper said. "I got a little go-go juice in the stash spot. I'll bring it along. Might be just the thing to cheer me up a little."

"Well hell yeah, Coop. Sounds like it's gonna be a celebration then." Davis offered up a fist bump, which Cooper returned half-heartedly.

"Maybe so. Might be the last one, though."

"Slow down, man. It ain't as bad as all that. People with kids have lives too. Or so I hear."

"Do they?" Cooper asked, not wanting an answer, but really more just wondering out loud. Davis shot him a grin and headed back out the front door.

CHAPTER SIX

It took some prodding and digging, but eventually Kirkpatrick was able to get the rednecks out at the Moore County Sheriff's Department to help him enough to figure out the incident his unsub "Coop" was involved in. Coop short for Cooper. The whole thing had him wondering if Dumas was pronounced "dumbass," but it yielded him two more names, Cooper Daniels and Trevor Davis, and the arresting officer's name, Chase Farrar. He was surprised he'd never come across this case before when looking into Sancho Watts's past, until he discovered the charge had been expunged and sealed. It took namedropping Weldon Robb's credentials to three people to finally get them ready to release the file.

After some more finagling, he was able to get Farrar's number. Apparently the man was now a sergeant at the Moore County Sheriff's Department. One thing Kirkpatrick knew for sure, he didn't trust these kinds of small town panhandle yokel cops, knew most of them to be racists, hopelessly stuck in a time that hadn't existed for fifty-odd years.

"This's Farrar," the man said by way of answering the phone, his thick country accent already engaging all kinds of stereotypes for Kirkpatrick. He explained the general outline of who he was, who he was working for and why, before asking Farrar if he remembered the case.

"Hell, yeah, I remember. Little hotshot sons of bitches

weaseled out of the whole thing. Was certain we could use some kind of Homeland thing to justify the search, too. You ask me that reefer them boys was carrying goes straight to funding Al Qaeda, and I told the judge so. Told the prosecutor, too, but the one guy, Watts, his daddy was some tough guy lawyer, come out here and run a mud hole through the goddamn prosecutor's ass."

Already Kirkpatrick didn't like this guy, but tried not to let it show in his voice. "Do you recall any details of how they came to end up in custody to begin with?"

"I do. They was over at the Frackin' Tavern, tying one on, when the Watts fella got all twisted off on some sort of drug. We was gonna test him but the boy's daddy was here faster than a greased monkey, shut all that shit down. Anyhow, he got to harassing a couple ladies in the bar and couple of good ol' boys from around here was about to stomp his ass. His other two partners managed to calm things down, but the bartender had already called us up by then. We met 'em at the door and initially took Watts into custody for P.I. Ran the other two's licenses, one was suspended and the other expired. Once we saw that we searched the car, found a couple pounds of dope, about five-thousand in cash."

"Were they getting in the car to leave or something?" Kirkpatrick asked, already knowing what had probably happened.

"No. We just figured one of the two had to of drove them there, so we searched it."

"Let me take a wild guess," Kirkpatrick said, struggling now to keep the heat out of his voice. He'd never had much use for cops that would railroad someone just because they thought they could get away with it. These small Texas towns operated on their own code, and hardly ever got called on it. "Watt's dad got them off on an illegal search, didn't he?"

"He did, the son of a bitch. Seems like no one gives a shit when these white boys is supporting terrorism, long as they got a good lawyer."

Kirkpatrick rolled his eyes, glad that didn't make any noticeable sounds, knowing good and well that the dope these rednecks took off Watts and company went to paying Colorado electricity bills and buying drugs to party with, not funding terrorists. He wondered how the man thought marijuana could make it all the way from Afghanistan when it was so much easier to either grow it yourself or get it from the next door neighbors in Mexico or Canada. He didn't mention it.

"Anything else you think I need to know about Watts or Davis?"

"Just that Watts got a mouth on him the size of The Palo Duro Canyon. I offered to fix it for him, but Chief straightened me out. I'd still pay good money for five minutes alone with that guy. The other two was model prisoners, though."

"Thanks for your time, Sergeant Farrar." Kirkpatrick hung up without waiting for a reply.

He ran the names and social security numbers of both Cooper Daniels and Trevor Davis, discovered they'd both grown up down in Conroe, figured they were maybe life-long partners in crime. If that was true, he had a hunch that Trevor Davis would probably show up in this thing somewhere along the way. With any luck he might pick up all three, but he was willing to sacrifice the other two if it meant he could nab Elroy Watts.

He didn't have much against marijuana, had always thought it should be legalized and regulated, instead of letting it fund drug cartels. He doubted these boys would even have a reason to send it to Texas if the lawmakers, Weldon Robb among them, were smart enough to regulate and tax it. At best, what the boys were doing amounted to tax evasion in his eyes, which was the federal government's problem, not his. He didn't have much use for the feds either, but he did intend to meet his mandate and bring Elroy Watts in. Maybe he could get to these guys and flip them on Watts before they delivered the load. It would be worth a try.

His next call was to Weldon Robb to see if he could work some connections and get Javi Perez on loan from Travis County as a special investigator to send down to Teller County. Robb hadn't called him back yet from their earlier conversation, which he took to mean the man hadn't had any luck arranging for a tail on Sancho Watts.

"Remind me why you need this fella in particular?" Robb asked when Kirkpatrick insisted on Javi.

"He's been working the case with me. Besides, he's about the only person over at Travis County who wants to help, trust me when I say that. Thing is, I need him granted special investigator status so he can come out of county with me."

Robb exhaled a deep breath into the phone. "Nothing but nonsense. You'd think The Great State of Texas could do better by lawmen. I'll call Sheriff Bridges myself and work it out. Asshole hates my guts though, so I'll have to lean on him pretty hard, I'd imagine. If it was his grandson I bet he'd burn down his own department looking for justice. Sure you can't just use one of the boys from the DPS?"

"I'm surprised they let you have me, honestly. I don't have to mention again that we're awash in grey area on this case, do I? Besides, I trust Javi, and he's a hell of a detective. You said you want justice for your grandson I believe he's a man that can help make sure that happens."

"Yeah," Weldon Robb said, his voice dripping with sarcasm. "Then where's the son of a bitch been all this time?"

Kirkpatrick wanted to remind the senator that law enforcement wasn't as easy as it looked, but didn't feel like taking any more abuse today. "Trust me, he's good, Senator," was all he said.

"Give me an hour and I'll call you back. And make sure you answer your phone, *comprende*?"

"I got it," Kirkpatrick said, wishing he could say a few more things, too.

The call came in not from Weldon Robb, but from Javi Perez.

"Kirkpatrick," Kirkpatrick said into the phone.

"Man your tacos sure come with some strings attached."

"I see the senator worked fast for once. Sorry to drag you back in, Javi, but I could sure use some competent backup with knowledge of the case. Shirley wasn't available, so they stuck me with you." Kirkpatrick smirked a little.

"I see how it is," Perez said, his own grin carrying in his voice. "It's all good, actually. I was kinda disappointed when it left our docket. I wanted to get the little fucker, too."

"Well let's go get him then. Glad to have you on board."

"Let's. But enough with the sweet talk. I don't have a choice either way. Bring me up to speed."

Kirkpatrick outlined the new information he'd uncovered, promised to send the file from Dumas over, along with the limited information he'd managed to dig up on Cooper Daniels and Trevor Davis. "I need you to pick up Watts's tail, starting ASAP, follow him down to Teller and get us a motel, something as cheap as you can find. Senator's orders. Maybe stick a transmitter on his truck or something, however you like to do it. Don't flash your badge around town or let him see you. Just keep a low profile, fill up on Whataburger or whatever Mexican food they got around, and wait on my call."

"You act like I was about to introduce myself to him and ask him out for margaritas, sheesh."

"Just being thorough. Make sure you know where he is at all times, Javi. Senator Robb is breathing down my neck on this deal, and making all kinds of vague threats about my future, too. I'm hoping for a straightforward controlled delivery, everybody goes down with their hand in the cookie jar, and Weldon Robb can sleep safe knowing his grandson has some vindication."

"Easy as pie," Javi said.

They outlined the details of what resources they might need. Javi asked if there was anything else, and when there wasn't, they signed off the call. Kirkpatrick cracked a beer afterward and sat back on the couch, tried to watch some baseball but couldn't get his mind off the case, as usual. He was starting to feel good about their prospects for catching Elroy Watts. This time the boy's father wouldn't be around to cover his ass. Sooner or later everyone's luck ran out. Criminals had to get lucky every single time they went out. Cops only had to be lucky one of those times.

Kirkpatrick finished the beer and opened another, already picturing the soft Caribbean sands of Mahahual. He could almost taste the chilaquiles at the Nacional Beach Club. Almost. He spent the rest of the night and about four more beers going over his notes again and again, making sure he knew every last bit of it by heart. You never knew when some tiny detail would make everything else fall into place. He'd learned to be thorough from his father, though he never matched the man's level in that department or any other that he could see. His father had been a cowboy, through and through. Kirkpatrick was a good cop, and a decent father, though he spent almost every night alone doing paperwork or reading case files, and had done the same back when his kids were still around the house. He doubted his father would be pleased to see just how few long-term relationships he'd actually built for himself in his life.

The job, or at least his obsession with it, had driven Melissa away after twenty hard-fought years of marriage. The job meant he didn't call his kids enough, and eventually they stopped calling him, too. The job meant he never slept well, didn't eat well, and almost never got to fish anymore.

And finally, for the first time in twenty years, he was starting to realize it. He needed a change. He needed a life. Soon as he wrapped Elroy Watts up in the net, he was taking a leave. Time to put all that saved and invested money to some real use, instead of just sitting on it like some old miser workaholic. It was fair to call him a workaholic, but one thing he knew for sure: He wasn't old. At least not yet.

CHAPTER SEVEN

The band was already going hard by the time Cooper and Davis arrived at Cervantes. They'd had to walk from the light rail station, missed the train they intended to ride down, meaning they were late. They both barely let the door guy get the stamp on their hands before pushing through into the club, the familiar odor of incense, weed and body oil filling Cooper's nostrils as soon as he crossed the threshold into the venue. That smell always brought back memories of his first show, scent being the one thing that stuck with him about the memory, even if he could never remember what the set list had been.

He and Davis had made up a story about a trip out to Don Whitaker's deer lease to divert their parents, though the story had been more for Cooper's folks, being that Davis's mom worked so much she might not even have noticed he was gone. They drove Cooper's two-door blue Ford Ranger up to Tulsa instead, smoking dope and eating boomers the whole way up, so that they arrived in Tulsa so high they had to do several laps around downtown before finding the parking lot.

Stepping out of the truck into that lot had been like stepping into a different world, one he'd never returned from. People beating on bongos, selling glass pipes from cases or peddling bootleg summer tour T-shirts, Bear Gone Fishin' stickers like the one he slapped on the back window of the truck afterward. Most of them doing more looking out for security and cops than anything else. Cooper learned later that bands sometimes sent their security out into the lots to mop up all the unauthorized merchandise. That night he also learned there was a whole other world out there, a travelling circus of sorts that surrounded what was already without question his favorite band: Widespread Panic.

People living out of their camper shells or even just bumming a ride from show to show, selling whatever it took to get there, whether drugs or burritos. It was like being on that lot had confirmed everything Cooper had ever felt but had been unable to put his finger on: the yearning to be free, the want of a life that wasn't so serious and structured and vanilla as what Conroe had to offer him.

The next summer, after he'd graduated high school, he did his first full tour, saw more of the country and made more friends than he'd ever dreamed, even if he didn't know most of their real names, and couldn't recall much about most of the cities now, beyond what went down in the parking lot before the shows. They'd funded the trip by scouring the fields outside of Conroe, looking for Cubensis mushrooms, eventually finding one that had plenty of them, and cultivating it by thumping each orange cap to release the spores back into the cow patties before picking it, even the prized unopened caps, which they took to calling bullets on account of their shape.

He learned that the ones with the blue veins were the strongest. Weeks later, when the black farmer who owned the land came barreling across his pasture in an old red Ford truck and cornered them with a shotgun, saying, "I don't know exactly what you plan to do with them mushrooms, but I got a good idea," they already had four pounds of dehydrated caps.

From there they just broke a few ounces down into eighths in each lot before the show, sold them and had more money than they knew what to do with, come show time each night. They even stayed in some nice hotels here and there, a habit that had held true all the way up until the present.

But tonight, at Cervantes for the thousandth time, weaving through the crowd, hugging and fist bumping with dreadie dudes he'd seen at dozens of shows, he had the feeling that all of it, this dream life he'd envisioned, was starting to crumble.

Truth was, Josie had been a part of it all for so long now that even if she dumped him it would never feel the same again. The thought that she even might dump him had him pouring more liquor down his throat and dipping the tip of a Parliament cigarette into his meager stash of blow more often than he should.

By mid-second set he was pretty well out of drugs. Davis started to fade after a while, too, and before long they were walking back to the light rail station, ready to head back to Cooper's place and crash.

It was on the way home that the idea hit Cooper as hard as if it had been the light rail train he was riding on. He and Davis were just kicking back, coming down off the cocaine as the train barreled along, drunk on whiskey and a few other things, when he looked out the window at the cityscape whipping by and saw the billboard. *Whatever your cargo, CRATES makes it easy. Delivery in all fifty states, do your moving with CRATES.* He nudged Davis, who had just about passed out, awake.

"You see that?" Cooper said.

"See what?" Davis replied. "My eyes was closed. I'm feeling a little woozy."

"The answer to our transportation problem, bubba. It

just hit me."

"Hit you?"

"Sober up and listen...CRATES."

"What, like the moving company?"

"Exactly like that. What we gonna do is have 'em drop one of them portable storage things off at the Jewell house, stuff one of the old couches up with the stash, toss the rest of the furniture in front of it and ship it down to Teller."

Davis sat up, alert now, eyes wide. "That's one hell of an idea, Coop. I actually can't believe we never thought of doing that before."

"Probably not safe to do all the time, but I bet we can do it once, no problem."

Davis frogged him in the shoulder and smiled. "You bet your ass we can. That's fucking genius. I was starting to sweat the drive down there, I'd be glad as hell not to have to ride dirty the whole way."

Cooper nodded. "Same. I'd imagine Josie will be glad to hear it, too. I'll get Sancho on the line tomorrow and figure out the rest of the details, but I feel like maybe we got it made now."

They got off the train at the Colorado Boulevard station and made their way back to Cooper's place as if they didn't have a care in the world, though somewhere deep inside, Cooper still had a bad feeling brewing.

Cooper's phone woke him out of a dead sleep hours later. He sat up, couldn't see anything but the lit-up phone vibrating on the coffee table next to the fraying green couch he'd been sleeping on for years. He hadn't used the bed at his place in so long it was piled under a foot of broken-down boxes, old HID lights, cartons of nutrients, and other general grow junk. Once his eyes adjusted, he didn't recognize the number.

"Yeah," he said when he answered. The chorus from *Arlene* blared into his ear through the receiver, and he had to hold it away from his face for a second.

"Coop?" what sounded like Sancho's voice yelled, sounding drunk, probably high, but definitely something. "That you, Senor Cooper?"

"Yeah, Sanch, it's me," Cooper said, rubbing the sleep from his eyes so he could check the time on the phone.

"You sleeping?"

"It's five a.m. Hell, yeah, I'm sleeping."

"When'd you all join the JV squad?" Sancho let the friendly jab hang in the air, then added, "I'm just fucking with you. My boy from T-town showed up and we been gettin' it. Was a time I could have expected you and Davis to be gettin' it, too."

"Hell, we were. Earlier," Cooper said, starting to wake up now. "Then we figured we done already got about all we was gonna get tonight, so we put it to bed."

"I understand. Anyhow, to business. This is my new burner, so save it. We got everything worked out. Can you be down in Teller in three days with the product?"

"I think so."

"Good. I'll meet you down there on Thursday and make the introductions all around. You gonna be shocked when you meet my guy, that's all I'm gonna say up front. I'm headed down day after tomorrow, do some fishing and chase some debutants around."

"That sounds good, I guess," Cooper said. "Anything I need to worry about in the meantime?"

"Shit, not on my end. It's all hook 'em Horns, big boy. Afterwards we can all catch up and have us a little party. Hang out with some East Texas girls."

Cooper hesitated. Sancho could get way too wild sometimes, and the last thing he needed was girls of any kind. He and Davis had already decided against hanging around after the deal to party, remembering how the last time they'd worked with Sancho it was the raging that nearly put them in prison. "Sounds good," was all he said, figuring he and Davis could just duck out of town after the deal and end up never having to talk to anyone about it again.

"All right then, you got the new number. Hit me up when you get down to Teller and I'll let you know where to bring the stash. Y'all can crash with me at my boy's lake house out on Lake Strongbow, if you want."

Cooper figured they'd hit a hotel, but didn't mention it.

"We'll work all that out when we get down there," he said, still not able to think very well.

Sancho rambled on about a few more things, Mexican restaurants they needed to try, barbeque and places to get a drink, before Cooper managed to get him off the phone. Afterward he wanted to go back to sleep, but the nerves had caught up with him about things with Josie, now that the alcohol and drugs had faded off. The confidence he'd felt just hours ago had become the first traces of a hangover, and suddenly he had the lingering suspicion that nothing in the world could ever be right again.

He thought about mixing a drink, then shuddered and thought better. Instead he packed the bong with the most Indica-dominant bud in his stash, some Skunk Six/Afghani, a strain he and his crew had taken to calling the Bin Laden after the cop who'd busted them in Dumas suggested that's who they were funding. Thinking about that night in Dumas again made him shiver.

Cooper cleared the tube a few times and sat back staring at the wall, not really thinking about anything now. And then he slept a long, hard sleep, one that had him waking up with drool on his shirt, but otherwise not having moved an inch in six hours.

He rubbed his eyes and got out of the chair, poked around in the kitchen, making coffee and trying to decide whether he should pick up some breakfast or head straight over to Josie's. It might piss her off if he seemed too hung over, given their conversation yesterday. It might also piss her off if he waited too long to come smooth things out.

Before he could make a decision, another problem stomped its way into his thoughts, one that gave him a sharp shot of adrenaline in the stomach. Using CRATES was a great idea, except, where were they going to have the crate delivered? He hadn't considered that in his inebriated state last night.

They could drop it at Sancho's guy's place, maybe, but that idea gave Cooper another flash of anxiety because it made him realize he didn't trust Sancho enough to do that. Sancho's guy probably wouldn't go for it anyway, too much risk. They needed somewhere to deliver it that they could control, a place where they could stash the load afterward and not have to feel exposed. What they needed was a storage unit.

He decided to head over to Josie's and use her internet to see what he could find. If he reserved one online, they could pay for it in person, unload the furniture into the unit as if there was nothing to it, then come back at night after the office was closed and get the stash out from inside the couch. Take it to a hotel or something. Give the owner a story about their new place falling through, tell him they're new to the area and in a bind, needed somewhere to keep their stuff that's cheaper than the CRATES storage lot. Maybe play up the corporate distrust angle or something.

He took a shower and shaved, put on some clean clothes. Once he had everything ready, he texted Josie to tell her he was coming by, waited ten minutes for a response before just saying fuck it and heading over there anyway. If he got lucky she might be at yoga, which would give him a chance to lock down a storage spot on the computer.

Cooper rolled through traffic in his grey Texas Edition Tundra, mind all over the place. Being from Texas had always been something he and Davis wore like a badge of honor, like all the other Texans he'd ever known. It was as close to having a tribe as they were ever going to get. Never mind that neither of them could stand the place when they actually spent any amount of time there.

Texans were wild, free people, and for all the things other people didn't like about them, Cooper had always sensed that people respected that part. Even so, he had to admit that the idea of going down there and doing business again scared the absolute shit out of him. It was almost like visiting a different country, and he couldn't think of a worse place to go to prison.

His uncle Charles, the black sheep in the family before him, had done five years in Huntsville, described it as "hotter than the sun and overrun with man-stink, so loud all the time you can hardly hear yourself think." Charles's crime had been that he couldn't stop drinking and driving until finally the law stopped it for him.

They had outlaws on his father's side stretching back to the Republic of Texas, but nobody ever talked about them, and he'd never met any himself. His father's only historical family discussion always centered around Cooper's great-great-great grandfather on his mother's side, Samuel Johnson, who'd been a hero at the Battle of San Jacento, then a famous Texas Ranger.

Cooper's parents had always been kind enough to pretend they didn't notice what he was up to, but he figured they had a good idea. He'd always suspected it was the reason they had never visited him in Denver in more than a decade of his living there. He returned the favor by rarely visiting Conroe, meaning he hadn't seen them in a couple of years now.

He pulled up to Josie's building and parked in the extra guest spot her father had rented in the building's garage so he'd have somewhere to park his car when he came up to see her. Her folks always drove up from Texas, never flew. Despite having more money than God, her father was too distrustful to fly commercial, and too cheap to buy a private jet. Instead they just miled-out their hundred-thousand-dollar Mercedes, coming to see their only daughter eight or ten times a year, which always gave Cooper a chuckle just based on the ridiculousness factor.

He'd always figured her parents didn't care for him. They'd never say that or anything else bad about him. They took him out to nice dinners with Josie, and even managed to avoid asking him what he was doing for work most of the time. But that amounted to nothing more than the smoke-screen of pure Texas courtesy. They were just waiting for her to get good and sick of him to make their move, which might be on the horizon if he didn't get his shit together.

The condo was empty so he flipped open Josie's MacBook and started searching for storage places in Teller on the outskirts of town. Cooper considered a few of the more reputable ones, but thought better of it. It made sense to look for something less professional, something run down, even. He settled on a small complex out on Old Teller Highway. It wasn't fenced for some reason and didn't look sophisticated enough on Google Maps to have cameras. It also seemed like the kind of place he could drop a CRATE overnight under the guise of moving to the area for a job.

He wrote down the number. He wanted to see if he could get by using a temporary credit card to book the place, use the surprisingly accurate fake Colorado driver's license his buddy Thomas had made for him one time at a Panic show in Vegas as a joke, under the name David Schools, also the name of Panic's bassist. Maybe he could register the pre-paid card under that name, pay cash for it, and at least have some cover on his trail.

The apartment's front door opened and Josie stepped inside wearing grey yoga pants and a bright yellow tank top, sweat glistening on her slender, tan arms. He always thought this was when she looked the most beautiful, though she would hardly let him near her when sweaty. Yoga tended to relax her, so Cooper had that working in his favor just now. She gave him a look that said she was neither surprised nor angry to see him.

"Hey, sweetie," Cooper said as he clicked off the search tab and stood up. "I figured you must have went to yoga."

She raised an eyebrow. "Figured it or planned for it?" she asked.

"Just figured. I been doing some thinking, and I wanted to talk with you about it."

"Way I heard it, you been doing some drinking, you and Davis both, down at Cervantes."

Cooper frowned, trying to figure who would have found that important enough to tell her. "That's true, too, we were. We were celebrating, actually, about the baby. What I wanted to tell you is that you're right, it's time to get out of all this nonsense. I've got Davis getting ready to sell off all the gear, get us a little cushion to prepare for everything." He hesitated, then added, "I'm excited about the baby."

Josie crossed her arms, but her blue eyes said he was starting to soften her. "Okay," she said.

"Okay what?" Cooper asked.

"Just, okay. I'm not sure what you're expecting here,

49

Cooper."

"I guess I was expecting you to be happy."

"I *am* happy, Cooper. I'm happy about this baby. And it's good that you're making the right decision. But the truth is this whole thing has me considering the future more than I ever have before."

"What's that mean?" he asked, already sort of knowing what would come next.

"It means that maybe it's time for me to move back closer to my family. This condo's no place to raise a baby, and no offense, but it isn't like you've got someplace else to take us all. I love you, Cooper, but I just get the impression that this might not be going anywhere. That *you* might not be going anywhere. I don't want to waste any more time, you know? I'm almost thirty. At my age my mother had two toddlers and was the president of The Junior League. I feel like I've got nothing, *we've* got nothing, and the fact is, yesterday you seemed content to keep having that nothing for the rest of our lives."

Cooper's cheeks warmed, so he took a deep breath. Fear shot up his side and slapped him in the left shoulder. He thought of a bunch of things he wanted to say, but all he said was, "Are you 'bout to break up with me, Josie?"

She looked away when he said it, which freaked him out. He could feel a wall going up between them, needed to say something before she put the last bricks in it, but didn't know what. She spoke instead.

"No. Actually, I don't even know. I'm confused, but I don't have the luxury of being confused anymore. I need to get myself ready to be a mother."

"That's what I'm over here trying to tell you. I'm trying to get myself ready to be a father, too. I can do this. Soon as I get back from this trip—"

She cut him off. "You see? Do you see why I'm confused?

You say you're ready for this, and then in the next sentence you say you're off to do some more criminal nonsense that could jeopardize the whole thing. I don't think you are ready, Cooper, I've got to be honest in saying that." She exhaled a deep breath, like it had been hard to finally say that to him.

Cooper held up his hands, shocked. "Whoa, let's just slow down a little and take a breath. I know how you're feeling, sweetheart, but—"

"But what? If you think you've got any idea how I'm feeling right now, then you don't know crap. You say that you're serious, but if you're really serious about being with me, about our baby's future, you need to let this *go*, Cooper."

"Let what go? You mean the crop?"

"Yes, Cooper, I mean the crop. Burn it or make earwax out of it and sell it locally. Heck, give it away, I don't really give a damn what it takes. But don't do this, don't go down to Texas with a car full of dope and get locked up before you even have the chance to be a father to our baby."

"That's just it. I figured all that out. We ain't gotta drive it now. We're shipping it down there stuffed into a couch, using CRATES. All we gotta do is drive down clean and make the deal in person, then head back with the cash. There's almost no danger."

"There's almost nothing but danger so long as you're dealing with Sancho Watts. Besides, this is exactly what I'm talking about, you just can't see it."

"Can't see what?"

"You can't see that above all else this is all about your need to play outlaw one more time. We could do without the money. Hell, my parents would *give* us the money, if we asked. Daddy could get you on running wire line or even running title back home. He told me he'd be happy to."

"I can't take that money from your father, Josie. It'd have more strings attached to it than Pinocchio. Besides, is that what you really want? The Woodlands? Nice brick house behind a gate, hot as the sun all summer, damn near everybody so goddamn conservative they can't tell an asshole from an elbow?"

"I don't know what I want. But I know I don't want this. I don't want to sit here working this job I won't even have in another few months, with my family a thousand miles away, waiting on you to grow up and become the man I know you could be."

Cooper took a deep breath. He could feel he was losing her, but he could also feel she didn't want to be lost. Maybe he ought to just let it go, donate the crop to the Greenfaith Cannabis Church up in Fort Collins and move on with his life.

But even as he said it to himself he knew he could never go through with it. If this was the last crop he was ever going to grow, he damn sure wanted to sell it. No way he was leaving that money on the table and asking her father to cover the gap, giving the man another reason to hold him in quiet contempt.

"I've—I just gotta do this one last thing, Josie. If you can't understand that, I don't know what to say. Don't ask me to take money from your folks. In some ways that'd be even worse than getting in trouble. It'd be like they own us, like they own *me*."

"Well you do what you've gotta do then. But I'm not promising I'll be here when you get back." She let those last words hang in the air in the way he'd only ever seen women do well. Cooper started to say something but changed his mind, afraid of what would come out of his mouth when he was this twisted off. He was dug in enough, no need to bury himself. Instead he picked up his phone off the table and headed for the door.

"So that's it, you're just gonna leave it like this?" Josie said from behind him.

Cooper hesitated, took a deep breath. "No. I just don't want to say anything stupid right now. I need to clear my head. I hope you can understand this is all a big change for me, too. I want to make it, but I can't get out dead broke. I promise everything will be okay. I hope you won't worry. But, sweetheart, believe me when I say I can't just walk around this money. I'll call you and let you know I'm safe when it's done. In the meantime, I hope you'll take the time to decide if you even want me around, because right now I get the feeling that maybe you don't, and that breaks my heart because I love you."

He walked out and shut the door before she could react. She needed time to cool off, he knew that. A couple of days and her whole worldview might change. She'd never been good at emotional situations, and being pregnant probably didn't make it any easier. Besides, at this point he wasn't totally sure keeping him around was in her best interest either. That tied his stomach up into an even tighter ball.

CHAPTER EIGHT

Kirkpatrick was still sitting in I-35 traffic in his personal vehicle, a beat-up white Toyota Tacoma, when he got the call from Javi Perez.

"Whadaya say, Javi?"

"You on your way down yet?" Perez asked.

"Sort of. Stuck in traffic on Thirty-Five. Anything special going on?"

"I don't doubt it. And yeah, you might say that."

Kirkpatrick waited for him to continue, realized Perez was gonna make him ask. "Okay, I'll bite. What might I say is special?"

Tailed him to a place called Vernon's BBQ to meet his friend. Think they're probably getting some drinks since they haven't been back outside in two hours or so."

Kirkpatrick beeped his horn at the car in front of him, who appeared to be busy texting instead of pulling forward. "What's special about that?" he asked as he changed lanes to get around the car.

"You aren't gonna believe who his contact out here is."

"I might. Try me."

"Bobby Burnell."

Kirkpatrick leaned forward. "You mean as in, Bobby Burnout?"

"I sure do."

"You sure?" Kirkpatrick asked.

54

"Sure as if he was carrying around his Heisman."

Kirkpatrick didn't say anything, his mind racing. Perez must have sensed it, because he added "I'll take your silence to mean you're playing connect the dots just like I did."

"Any chance he's not involved? I kind of like the kid, or anyway, I did when he was winning championships at UT."

"I've seen bigger coincidences. But you remember his family's reputation. It was all over the news back when he burned out of Carolina."

"Shit. I know his uncle Troy did some time over in the LeBlanc unit for trafficking. Grandfather was supposedly knee deep in racketeering back in the oil boom days, but no one ever caught him. Teller County has their own version of justice, or so I hear."

"What I heard too."

"All right, well just stay with 'em, I guess," Kirkpatrick said, already feeling like he was stepping knee-deep into something he'd be better off not dipping a toe in. "We can rendezvous once I get down there. You grab us a room somewhere?"

"Sure did. Tell Senator Robb thanks for not splurging on individual rooms, that was a nice touch."

Kirkpatrick ran a hand through his hair. "Believe me, I'll be as happy to untangle from the cheap son of a bitch as you will once we tie this booger off. Let's hope it don't keep getting complicated."

Perez snickered into the phone.

"What?" Kirkpatrick asked.

"There I was thinking I'd already gotten untangled until you came calling. Next time you bring tacos to the station, I'm having Shelly throw you out."

"She wouldn't do it. Girl's smitten with me."

"Probably true. Never gave me the time of day. I thought

it was because I'm Mexican. Now I can see she's just got bad taste."

"Ha ha. Well anyway, adios, amigo, see you shortly," Kirkpatrick said.

"Drive safe." Perez hung up.

Kirkpatrick turned up the radio, tuned it over to The Ranch, glad that he still had an hour or so before he could no longer pick it up and would be forced to listen to whatever garbage pop music the people out in Nashville were passing off as country music to the local-yokel stations out in the sticks.

His daughter Amy loved that stuff, rolled her eyes at him every single time he'd tried to set her straight with some Waylon. Even Willie didn't sway her. Damn girl grew up and stopped giving a damn what he thought about anything at some point, pretty much. Maybe she learned it from her mother.

His son Jason wasn't a whole lot better. Since the boy moved off to Seattle, he barely ever heard from him, hadn't seen him in person in three years. At least Amy stopped in to see him when she came to town for Christmas, though she always stayed with her mother and stepfather in their obnoxious house out in Westlake.

His ex-wife Melissa must have decided when she divorced him that it was the lack of money that killed their marriage, rather than Kirkpatrick's lack of attention, because she drove her bus straight at that bigshot real estate attorney Ronnie Potts, damn near ran the fuck over him.

Potts might as well have been the human incarnation of what Kirkpatrick hated about attorneys. Diamond cufflinks, pearl-colored Mercedes that cost more than Kirkpatrick made in a year. Fake smile that looked like someone etched it in ivory. What a fucking cheese dick. He figured she probably aimed on purpose for the guy he was most likely to despise.

Half an hour later Kirkpatrick turned off the interstate and headed east out into the slight rolling hills and tall trees of the piney woods. Prettiest part of the state, which seemed like a real waste when you realized how backward some of the people living there were. Teller County in particular had a reputation for corruption in law enforcement, he'd read a book about it, lucky to even get a copy after the local socialites made it their mission to destroy every single copy in print.

Sheriff Jack Gables ran a tight ship, had even survived being chin deep in the scandal outlined by the book Kirkpatrick had read. He had been forewarned that outside intervention in Teller County was almost never treated with any degree of welcome, which was why he'd called Weldon Robb off from asking anyone local for help. He was determined to wrap Watts up without help from anyone else but Javi Perez. His own department sure as hell wasn't going to devote any resources to Weldon Robb's revenge mission, even if they had allowed him Perez, which was, as much as anything, a Hail Mary attempt to get rid of him for good.

It would take more than tacos, flirting, and lame jokes to squeeze so much as a head nod out of the local sheriff's department in Teller County anyway or so he'd been told.

CHAPTER NINE

Bobby Burnell was in it now, he guessed. Could have been an NFL star, rookie of the year even, had things gone a little bit different. Had he *decided* to make them different. Back at Lee High School they'd called him Bobby Bigtime, everybody sure he would end up a star, a real, bona fide pro. And he did, for a moment—signed with University of Texas, did one year as a redshirt, fucking won the national championship as the starter two years later. Heisman Trophy too, and all the pussy he could eat.

Problem was he also made a name for himself on the Austin party scene. Half the time he'd wake up with a girl whose name he didn't remember, the other half, two. Either way he'd have a hangover the next morning that would kill an entire Southern Baptist congregation, and occasionally a bad case of crabs. Eventually he had to start drinking a couple of warm beers in the shower every morning to stave off the shakes. But it never affected his play.

Not until he got drafted by the Carolina Panthers, which would have meant big, big money, had his accident not happened. First-round money. Not that he ever saw any of it. Nearly wrapped his brand new Camaro around a tree out on Highway 14 not two days after he signed. That should have killed him. Flipped it five times across some pasture and landed upside down next to an oil derrick that kept pumping away like nothing had happened.

He was drunk, as usual. Would have escaped totally unharmed, except the middle finger on his throwing hand got tangled up in the custom steering wheel and torn right off. Bled like a son of a bitch. Hurt even worse. Might have bled all the way out if Melanie Freeman hadn't been with him. Girl escaped with little more than a cut on her scalp that turned her forehead purple where it had hit the side of the car. Barely eighteen years old and came within inches of death, still had the sense to put a tourniquet on his forearm.

No way to put one on his career though, throwing hand all fucked to hell. It still bothered him that they were never able to find the finger. Probably got eaten by a coyote or some shit. Carolina withdrew their offer before he even left the hospital. The news media had a field day, started calling him Bobby Burnout, following him around everywhere so bad that he had to hole up in the family lake house, have people bring him food. And liquor, of course.

Now, a year and some change later and finally off probation, here he was out of options and finally joining the family business, something his father had never wanted for him back before he passed. People had been calling the Burnell family the East Texas Mafia for years, though the truth was they were just a bunch of good ol' boys willing to do what it took to get what they wanted, with the money and influence to back that up.

When Sancho told him about a bunch of fine-ass weed coming down from Colorado, he figured this to be his big chance. Hook the good ol' boy network up with a cheap dope supplier up Colorado way, take his cut of each shipment. Show he was good for more than throwing a football and pounding whiskey. Act casual afterward, telling Uncle Troy that he had hookups, too.

Tell him how they used to hang out at Sancho's family ranch a few miles down I-35, toward Kyle, after coach Brown forbade him from drinking. How Sancho had looked out for him, brought chicks out there for him to get down with. He'd leave out the part about everyone tripping balls on Sancho's mushroom goo, some kind of magic mushroom extract one of the hippy's friends cooked up.

His uncle Troy hated psychedelics, on account of a trip to the ER as a teenager after he took some wild East Texas mushrooms and lost his shit, thought he was dying. Guy moved cocaine like Pablo Escobar and still managed to take a moral stand against drugs somehow. Bobby was tired of being stuck in Teller on the weekends after playing apprentice for Troy's psycho ass all week. When he heard Sancho was back in town he figured he'd go pay Sancho a visit, hook something up, have a damn good time in the process. When this weed deal fell in his lap it felt like fate. Nobody had told him a life of crime would involve so much running to pick up Troy's lunch from El Charito or Vernon's BBQ.

And now here they were, sitting at Vernon's BBQ, the deal on the way into town. This could change everything, if he played it right. Bobby rubbed his middle finger stub while he waited for Sancho to come back from the bar with the next round. He liked that about Sancho. The guy always wanted to be the one hooking everything up, life of the party.

"Can you still feel that shit, like a phantom pain or whatever the fuck they call it?" Sancho asked as he set down the frosty pitcher of Shiner Bock.

Bobby put his hand in his lap out of instinct, still embarrassed to have people acknowledge it, like they were acknowledging what a fuck-up he was. "Sometimes," he said, then nodded yes when Sancho gestured with the pitcher to ask if he wanted a refill.

"I've never even had stitches," Sancho said. "Although I

damn near blew my ass up one time making butane hash."

"Why they call it butane hash?" Bobby asked, not having heard of that before.

"'Cause it's made with butane. You've had it, probably just called it earwax."

"Oh, yeah." Bobby nodded and took a drink of his beer, feeling a little self-conscious about having had to ask, and also because the one time he'd smoked earwax he'd gotten so high he had to throw up. But even still, his curiosity got the better of him. "What do they use the butane for?"

"They blow it through the trim that's left over after they harvest and manicure the bud, stuff it into a pipe or other similar cylindrical thing and shoot butane from a can right down through it. The butane is cold as fuck, and oily. Fats and oils absorb THC really well. Shit drips out the other end with all the THC mixed in with it. Then they take it and cook the butane back off in a double boiler, and what's left is the hash."

"I still don't get it," Bobby said. "Then how'd you almost blow yourself up?"

"You kidding?" Sancho said. "All that butane in the air, fucking hot water heater or some other thing makes a tiny spark and *boom!*, whole place goes Al Qaeda."

"When are your boys gonna be down here?" Bobby asked, feeling nervous about ducking out on working with his uncle Troy today, needing to buy the time to get the deal done, becoming an asset rather than a liability. Troy had never met a man he didn't think had gotten too big for his britches, so Bobbly needed to play it just right. If Bobby's father were still alive, things would be much easier, but he'd been dead since Bobby was a junior in high school, heart attack at forty-eight.

"Sometime tomorrow night, I think," Sancho said. "Long drive down here from Denver. Most people split it up so they don't ever have to drive at night. Less chance of getting rolled that way. You blend in with the daytime traffic."

Bobby had seen some of Sancho's friends from out on the Widespread Panic tour, had a hard time believing any of them could blend in anywhere.

"These guys born and raised in Colorado?" he asked, trying to get a feel for what they might be like, whether he needed to be worried.

"Nah. From down here, originally. Beaumont or some-where, I think. Something like that. I know what you're stressing over, kid. Don't worry. They mostly look like good ol' boys, not hippies. Relax and have a good time, it's all good. It's good to be hanging with you again, bro." Sancho tilted his beer for a toast.

"Who's worrying?" Bobby said as the bottles clanked, worrying like a motherfucker right when he said it. "Let's head down to the square after this and get us some more drinks."

CHAPTER TEN

Cooper and Davis met the CRATES guy at the scheduled time, signed the necessary forms, and then sat back and watched as he maneuvered the custom delivery truck into the driveway and dropped off the eight-foot container. It took some finagling and a fifty-dollar bill to persuade him to come back and pick it up the same day, which apparently was against policy.

"What's the rush?" the driver, an aging man with a fat belly and curly, greying hair, had asked.

Cooper had given him a story about his old lady kicking him out, telling him that whatever was left might get set on fire when she got home from work. Really not that far from the truth, beyond the fire. It did feel like Josie was kicking him out of their life together.

The driver left after promising to return two hours later. Cooper and Davis got to work. They'd spent the whole morning weighing out the harvest and sealing it up in half-pounds, using a vacuum sealer, careful to only seal the bags, rather than suck out the air and compress them. They double-layered the Food Saver bags to make sure there was no smell, either, then fit them into the hollowed-out back of the couch. When they finished, Davis used a staple gun to reconnect the fabric along the couch's backside where they'd pulled it up, putting a layer of flattened cardboard boxes between the stash and the fabric so you couldn't feel them in there from the outside.

Afterward they loaded the couch up into the CRATE with its back to one wall, took a break to have a beer, then stacked the recliner Cooper had picked up from Goodwill a few years ago on top of it, along with some boxes of old stuff he had been meaning to donate to Goodwill but had never gotten around to.

When they finished it looked pretty much like a single guy's shitty roster of stuff. They both doubted anyone would be looking in the CRATE anyway, fast as it needed to move.

An hour later the CRATES' driver showed back up and dragged the CRATE back up onto the truck, using the specialized lift connected to his flatbed rig. Cooper smiled and shook his hand. Soon as the guy was gone they hit the road, Cooper ready to get the thing done as quickly as possible.

They drove straight through from Denver to Teller, fifteen hard hours, switching off every couple of hours as they made their way across the Kansas prairies, terrain so flat you could see for miles, and then on down into Oklahoma. They listened to old Panic shows and talked through memories of life out on the road as they drove, got a little nostalgic, then shook it off and turned the music back up. Loud.

In Oklahoma Davis insisted they stop at the very first Whataburger they saw. Not that Cooper needed persuading. Two double Whataburgers with spicy ketchup and pickles later they made it across the Red River into North Texas. They wound their way off the highway and out into the piney woods, and eventually wound up in Teller about seven in the morning, Cooper so tired behind the wheel he was worried about maybe having an accident, driving off into the ditch and making all his problems moot without solving anything.

They pulled into the first motel they saw after getting off the highway, The Rose Motel. It was a shithole, no question about that. But they were both so tired they didn't care, decided as long as it had a bed and a roof they'd survive. They'd stayed at worse, anyway, out on the road. Back before they really started balling and trying to outdo each other on fancy hotels, meals, weed, everything really. That was the thing about going out on tour—sometimes you stayed in the nicest hotel within fifty miles, and sometimes the nicest hotel within fifty miles was a shit-box like this one.

They slept it off in room 223 on two double beds with ratty old patterned spreads that they both peeled off onto the floor before even setting their bags down. Cooper's spread had a burn mark that went through the spread into the blanket below, meaning the sheets probably hadn't been changed. Cooper didn't exactly remember going to sleep, just sort of woke up however many hours later, dazed, thinking about Josie and his coming baby again. He checked his phone but Sancho hadn't called yet, despite it being almost noon.

This constantly waking-up thing was new to him. Up until a few days ago he'd always prided himself on being able to sleep anywhere, anytime. It had often been a gift in this lifestyle, the ability to catch some floor space in some stranger's hotel room, or perhaps just sleep it off in the car at a rest stop.

Davis was the kind of guy who normally had a hard time going to sleep, but once he got there he went dead to the world. Cooper had fucked with him many times over the years because of it, drawn a dick on his face, piled everything in the room on top of him, bags, chairs, all of it. Davis never got angry, that's what Cooper had always loved about him.

They'd run in a larger group of friends at certain points, but often found them selfish, hedonistic even, just not really the type of people to care about anyone but themselves. Cooper had manners, as did Davis, and it had always made them both uncomfortable when friends acted entitled toward hotel staff, rude or out of control, which was pretty damn often, thanks to the drug buffet their crew usually had around. After a while they started travelling solo, sometimes bringing along Josie and Davis's ex, Rema, but a lot of times just the two of them, road warriors, jamming good tunes, eating and sleeping where they pleased, and always able to get away from the crew when moods turned sour from lack of serotonin.

They understood each other, which meant they seldom fought, like brothers who actually got along instead of fist-fighting.

Cooper sat up and looked around the dark motel room, afternoon light just starting to seep through the curtains. His back was still stiff from sitting in the car, and though he didn't feel old, he had to admit that he never used to get stiff no matter how far they drove.

He grabbed his Nalgene bottle off the table and stumbled through the dim room to the sink, filled it. The water tasted like a lake, nothing like the clean-tasting water that came out of the tap in most parts of Colorado. By the time he returned to bed he was worrying again about Josie, picturing her already packing up, alone, heading down to The Woodlands to live at her parents' place.

He needed to do something, because his life was at a crossroads. He couldn't imagine living without Josie. He also couldn't imagine ever leaving Colorado for Texas again. He wished he had some herb to spark up right then, put him back to sleep. They'd decided to roll totally clean on the way down, so they could drive as fast as needed and not have the anxiety that even a small amount of weed could bring in more conservative states.

Eventually he drifted back off to sleep to the sound of traffic picking up out on Finney Avenue. There was no denying that today would be a big day, the kind that could either make or break his entire life. He just wanted to get it done and get back home to his soon-to-be family. He could figure out everything else after that.

CHAPTER ELEVEN

Kirkpatrick was on the outskirts of Teller when the phone lit up again, displaying Javi's number.

"Just pulling into town, Javi, what's up?" Kirkpatrick asked.

"You're not gonna like it," Javi said as a greeting.

Kirkpatrick gripped the wheel tighter. "Lay it on me, I guess," he said.

"Our man just got picked up by the local boys, DWI."

"You're fucking shitting me."

"Wish I was. I'm tailing them down to the station right now. Was our man Watts that was driving, too, instead of Bobby Burnout. Did you know that we picked Bobby up no less than four times for DWI when he was at UT? Sheriff kept having to round everyone up and remind them he'd can every single one of us if the shit got out. Lucky for him damn near everybody there was a Horns fan. Me, I just don't like making waves at work."

"I'd heard the rumors. Kid had the golden touch, you know how it goes. Being good at football is as close as a man can get to royalty around here."

"I guess. Anyhow, I don't want to worry you, but they took them both downtown. You want me to go in and talk to the arresting officer before they book him? I wouldn't be surprised if our man had some sort of bullshit in his pocket. He stopped off at Burnell's house and dropped his bags off when he got into town, but you never know."

Kirkpatrick sighed. "Nah, I'll take care of it when I get there. Wouldn't that be peachy if he did have something? Probably roll over on his Colorado buddies and squirm out of everything again."

"Senator Robb will pop a hemorrhoid if he does."

"Or pop one of mine. Anyway, I'll meet you at the motel. Rose Motel, right?"

"That's the one, room 124."

"All right, I should be there in twenty minutes at the most. We can go over everything then. I'd hate to have these boys know we're digging around in their sandbox, but I don't want them fucking it all up, either, so I may have to go in and level with the sheriff."

"Sounds good. See you in a bit then," Perez said as he hung up.

Kirkpatrick needed to figure out how to play this. Maybe they'd get lucky and Watts would be clean, get released for the DWI and get back to dealing. But then, why'd they take them both in? For sure Watts's daddy wasn't going to come charging in, threatening to sue the pants off everyone in sight, this time. If the dumbass got locked up for a few days the whole deal could go south.

Kirkpatrick looked down and realized he was speeding. Just then he remembered Teller County was dry, wished now he'd picked up a sixer for the two of them to drink when he got there. It was late enough that he'd like to just guzzle a couple of cold ones and go on to bed. If there was one thing dealing with Watts had taught him, it was that anything that could go wrong would go wrong. Kid must have sold his soul, as many times as he'd managed to avoid prosecution. Weldon Robb would have Kirkpatrick stationed out in Marfa somewhere if he didn't make this stick. Time to put the game face on.

Twenty minutes later he pulled into an empty spot next to a rusted old Dodge pickup. Javi's car, a charcoal grey Camaro, was parked a few spaces down. Kirkpatrick wondered how Javi had managed to follow anyone in that mean-looking car without being noticed. He probably should have asked Javi to drive something different, but too late now. Anyhow, how picky could he be after asking the man to use his own vehicle for professional business?

He could see Javi Perez laid up shirtless on the far bed from the door as he passed the window. Javi saw him, too, and came to the door to let him in.

"How was the drive down?" he said as he opened the door. Then, remembering he was shirtless, added, "Hotter than hell in this room when I first got in. AC is running now."

"Look like you been working out, Javi."

"Six-pack curls. I jog a couple miles a week, but that's it. Just in the blood, I guess."

Kirkpatrick dropped his bag on his bed, sat down. "Anyhow, tell me more about our man. What's the status?"

Perez resumed his position on the bed and said, "They took 'em in the station, I didn't want to go any closer than that. It's not too far from here, actually. I'd imagine they're booking them as we speak, probably keep them there overnight."

"How you think we should play it? Go in and make friendsies with the locals, or play cool and see about tailing him when he gets out?"

"I'm not sure, but you're the boss."

"I've heard all kinds of bullshit about this county, none of it good. Had a partner when I was down in Houston who used to work out here, said they ought to flip the roles in Teller County, let the criminals police the cops. Less crime that way."

70

"Good ol' boy mafia. Like you said, I think we wait and see. You want, I can play skip tracer, go down and see if they still got the kid bright and early."

"I like the idea," Kirkpatrick began, "but let me do it. In fact I think I'm gonna do it right now. Probably have some rookie on the desk for the overnight shift, might get something out of him. You get some sleep, might be you're gonna be back on surveillance here pretty quick." Kirkpatrick got off the bed and picked up his keys. "Meantime, I'll see what I can find out. Now give me some directions down to the station."

CHAPTER TWELVE

"Boy, you got a hard-on for trouble, don't ya?" Sheriff Jack Gables sat back in his swivel chair, arms crossed over the round silver star on his chest, giving Bobby the cop eye like he wasn't the biggest gangster in the region himself. "I already called your uncle, sounds like he's coming down ready to slap you around. You skim that cocaine we pulled off your boy from Troy, or what? Might as well tell me, you know you gonna tell Troy anyway."

"Jack, I got nothing to say until they get here." Bobby crossed his arms, but it made him feel more like a defiant child than a tough guy.

"Reach again, boy. That's Sheriff Gables to you. And nothing to say, ain't that a first? Back at UT you couldn't shut the fuck up. Look like you back down to size now, though. Your uncle Zach always said you was way too big for your britches. 'All foot and no balls,' is how he put it."

"Yeah? He call from prison to tell you that?"

Gables stood up, leaned across his desk so close that Bobby could smell the Copenhagen on his breath. "I dare you to say one more smartass word, Bobby Bullshit, I'll smear you on the carpet there like the little shit stain you are. Your uncle Zach's a real man, doing his time and keeping his mouth shut. You ought to try it, things might go better for you if you did."

"Look, *Sheriff.* I ain't got anything to say until Uncle

72

Troy gets here. He'll probably smear me for you when he does, anyway."

Bobby was pissed off about getting picked up, but knew better than to push Jack Gables much further. His uncle Troy had worked as much for Gables as he had for their family operation in recent years. Gables had been Teller County Sheriff for more than thirty years, and been crooked as hell for every single one of them. Not so much as a gram of anything was sold in Teller County unless it went through Jack Gables first. The ones who didn't abide by that had a funny way of ending up drowned in Lake Strongbow, if they ever turned up at all.

It didn't take a genius to tell Gables was sniffing around Bobby right now, looking to see if he was hustling behind Troy's back. Gables, like his uncle, had a way of sniffing out even the tiniest whiff of deception, probably why he'd managed to stay sheriff so long, in spite of the rumors. Bobby needed to persuade Troy to have them forget the bag of cocaine they'd picked up off Sancho and let them both go—without either Troy or Gables finding out about the weed deal yet.

No question that Gables would want a piece of that, and not just today, but always, afterward. Nobody would give Bobby an ounce of credit for setting it up unless he completed it on his own.

When Troy showed up he'd have to act contrite, apologize, whatever it took to get all three of them on their way as soon as possible. Not like Gables actually gave a shit about the coke, he just didn't like the idea of cocaine he hadn't gotten his cut of popping up in someone's pocket, especially if that someone was in the car with his business associate's nephew. Deputy Desmond Charles had brought them in, and as far as Bobby could tell, Charles was angling to fill Zach's former shoes as resident lackey.

Bobby would have to come up with something good to tell Troy. Troy was too sharp not to smell that he was up to something. No way his friend from Austin came down to Teller just to party. Bobby didn't like the idea of having to tell Troy about the deal up front, but it might end up being easier than trying to sneak around him, once he was suspicious. Troy was as likely to let him sit his ass in jail for a couple days as he was to take him home, anyhow.

Half an hour later Troy came through the door, chest puffed out beneath an American Fighter T-shirt, designer jeans so tight they could have been painted on, his slicked back hair making him look like a wannabe Mexican pimp. Troy had done some amateur kickboxing back in the day, and now he fancied himself a mixed martial arts promoter in addition to being Teller County's resident tough guy. When his uncle was Bobby's age, he'd developed a repute-tion for pistol-whipping people for even the smallest trans-gressions, even had to do a stretch after he whipped on the wrong socialite's son on the side of the highway one night. Most people steered clear of Troy after that.

Back then Troy had been as country as they come. Star linebacker on the football team, but never good enough to make college, though he had the size. Now he plucked his eyebrows and had Bobby drive him around in a pearl white Escalade that made them look like they thought East Texas was Hollywood.

Mad as Troy looked, Bobby was glad it wasn't Zach, his father's youngest brother. Big Zach had never hesitated to slap him upside the head for stupidity. Being three hundred pounds of stocky, drug-slinging cowboy, there never was much Bobby could do but take it. Zach had only been his father's half-brother, hence the last name Ellis, rather than Burnell.

But the half he'd gotten was the mean part, him the product of an affair with some stewardess, who promptly dropped him off after he was born and left town. Always had a chip on his shoulder about that. Bobby's grandfather had forced everyone to accept Zach as one of the family, even his own wife Sherry, who was so beat down by then she would have accepted just about anything she was told to.

Zach had always been second in command to Troy, though. Troy had more smarts. But what Zach lacked in intelligence he made up for in violence. Except now the violence had caught up with him and he'd had to limp off to prison for two or three years, all on account of out-of-county bullshit he was caught up in with Gables, who promptly washed his hands of it by promising Zach big things when he got out. That, and promising to pull some strings to get him paroled ASAP. About that time everybody went back to being happy that Zach hadn't been a true Burnell, though it hadn't done much to silence the speculation around town that the whole family was crooked.

Back when Troy had done his stretch after pistol-whipping James Ambrose, the son of a man with too much money to be pistol-whipped, people had looked the other way out of fear. But folks had been speculating about the Burnell family being criminals for three generations, really, and they were right.

Lately Troy had insisted they keep a low profile, move nice and smooth until the FBI stopped poking around the county. Bobby figured it was Gables's orders. Every few years the feds came down and looked into rumors of corruption at the Teller County Sheriff's Department, but nothing ever came of it.

Gables stepped outside his office to speak with Troy before he could come in, closed the door behind him so that Bobby couldn't hear what they were talking about.

Bobby took in the office: criminal justice degree from Texas A&M on the wall behind the desk; a bunch of bullshit community service awards surrounding it; and a display of classic gunfighter pistols mounted to the wall, not unlike the Colt .357 Lawman Gables carried in his holster, always the quintessential old west sheriff at heart. Bobby waited for Troy to come in for a couple of minutes before the door swung open and his uncle stepped inside, sat down without saying hello.

"So?" Bobby said, once it became apparent Troy wasn't going to speak first.

"So, what?" Troy replied, pretending to pick dirt from his perfectly manicured fingernails.

"So, we gonna sit here and clean our nails or you getting me and my boy out of here?"

Troy smiled, didn't look up. "Seems to me I'm up here specifically to clean the dirt out from under my nails. Of course, as usual, I'm related to the dirt, so I ain't got no choice."

"Come on, Troy, be serious. We was just having some fun. My buddy came through town visiting. I didn't realize the guy was being so careless with his speed."

"What about the cocaine? Thought I told you to lay off that shit for good."

Bobby frowned, looked down at the table. He needed to tread carefully here. "I have been, really I have. I didn't know he was gonna bring any along. Matter of fact, I barely had any, it was mostly for him."

Troy leaned his tattooed forearms on the desk, the twinkle in his eyes replaced with a hard stare now. " I tell you to keep it down to just a little drugging or to cut it out completely?"

Bobby sighed. "All right, you got me. I'm sorry, I shouldn't have done it. Believe me I'm not happy about you

76

having to come up here and talk to Jack Gables to get us out."

"Who said anything about getting you out? And who's *us*?"

"Come on, Troy. I know they ain't gonna charge me. Might as well have them bring my boy Sancho along with us, too. They can keep the blow, I won't touch it ever again, I swear."

Troy sat back, crossed his arms in front of his chest and didn't say anything else. Bobby couldn't decide if he was thinking things over or fucking with him, as usual. Finally Bobby couldn't take it, spoke up. "Seriously, Troy, I can't just leave my boy to rot. Can you please talk to Jack and get them to release him with me?"

"Why?" Troy said.

"I told you. He's my friend."

Troy stood up, moved over to the door and opened it to reveal Jack Gables standing outside, waiting. "Have nice stay, Bobby," Troy said. "Might be that a couple days of hanging around the cellblock will do you some good."

"Come on, Troy. Quit fucking around," Bobby said.

"I'll quit fucking around when you get ready to," Troy said.

"What's that supposed to mean?"

Gables spoke up this time. "It means that if you want me to let y'all out of here, you better stop bullshitting your uncle and tell us what you and your nappy-headed friend in there are really up to, boy."

So that was it. Bobby should have known. His uncle was sharp, that's why he'd been the one to take over when his grandfather, Gerald Burnell, died. Gables was even sharper, the reason he'd survived so long being crooked.

Bobby sighed, realized he'd have to come clean if he wanted the deal to go down. "I was gonna tell y'all after it was done," he began. "I got one hell of a deal set up. That's a potential long-term partner you're about to leave setting in that room across the way."

Troy sat back down and motioned with his hand for Bobby to continue. Bobby looked around, unsure. "Maybe we'd better talk about it once we leave?"

"Why?" Troy asked. "Jack's on the team, just like you."

"It's just..."

Gables and Troy stepped inside the office, closed the door. Troy stood above Bobby, leaned down into his face. "We all in this shit together, Bobby, right? I ain't got time for all this bullshitting around. Talk or stay here and think it over."

Bobby sighed, leaned back in his chair and tried not to glare at Jack Gables, who looked about ready to curb-stomp him. He outlined the whole deal for them, the thirty pounds of high-grade smoke, the meeting with the Colorado guys tomorrow, all of it. By the end of the conversation he could tell Troy wasn't as mad as before. Problem was, he couldn't tell anything else about what either Troy or the Sheriff were thinking.

CHAPTER THIRTEEN

Kirkpatrick pulled up and parked across the street from the Teller County Jail, a boxy, four-story beige brick building that would look as at home in Stalinist Russia as it did on a town square in a small East Texas town like Teller. He knew from memory that the place had a caged-in basketball court on top, though it wasn't visible at night. He pushed through the swinging glass doors into a lobby that probably hadn't been updated since the 1960s, all VCT tile and concrete walls, an aging, chest-high desk running across the back, where the desk clerk sat.

And what a desk clerk she was, short blonde hair in a bob cut with crystal blue eyes that looked up to meet him as he approached.

"May I help you, sir?" she asked.

"I sure hope so," Kirkpatrick started in, trying to work the charm. "I'm working for a bondsman out of Austin, been trailing a guy who stiffed him on the court date, heard he might have gotten picked up by you guys this evening. I was hoping to see what the deal was, if y'all got him, or what?"

"So you *heard*, did you?" she said.

Kirkpatrick hesitated, sensing she wasn't buying his story already. "Well, sort of. I came to Teller looking for him. Someone tipped me off he might have gotten picked up on a DWI or something. Name's Elroy Watts."

The desk clerk, Officer E. Meadows by her nametag, didn't even look at her computer.

"Which bondsman?" she asked.

Kirkpatrick couldn't explain why, but she made him feel exposed in some way. "Charlie Kauffman, Railroad Bail Bonds," he lied, hoping old Charlie was still in business back in Austin, or better, that she didn't know who he was.

"And you are?" she said, her face all business, betraying nothing.

"Russell Kirk," he said.

Again she didn't check the computer. After a second he realized she wasn't going to.

"So," he said, "think you could check if he's here for me?"

"Depends," she replied, still holding his gaze.

"On what, exactly?"

"On whether you're ready to stop feeding me bullshit and tell me what agency you're from or if you want to keep riding that garbage bondsman story."

Kirkpatrick kept her gaze too, but she didn't flinch. He exhaled a deep breath, looked away and smiled. "It's that obvious, huh?" he said.

"I sure wouldn't put you up for any undercover work if I was your boss. Now tell me, who are you really, and what do you really want?"

Kirkpatrick sighed. "Girl, you could stare down a wild boar. Got me over here shook. I'm Russ Kirkpatrick with the Texas Rangers." Kirkpatrick took out his badge and showed it to her for confirmation.

"That's better. Texas Rangers, huh? You mind telling me what has you in Teller County looking for a DWI at midnight on a Friday night? I don't mean to pry, but Sheriff Gables can be a pretty big boar himself when he finds out other agencies are operating within the county without giving him a head's up."

Kirkpatrick leaned on the counter, trying to be casual. Girl had eyes like drill bits, no question. "It's like this. I'm working a special assignment at the behest of State Senator Weldon Robb, which is, in itself, a long headache of a story. No offense to you and yours, but we've been trying to wrap this knucklehead up for a while, with very little luck. To tell you the truth he was just getting ready to hang himself out to dry until he managed to get locked up on this dewey. I would have contacted y'all, I was just afraid inter-agency politics might get messy and throw a kink in the plan. All I'm really trying to see is what all they've got on our guy, and whether he's gonna stay locked up long enough to spoil our plans with him. That's it, as transparent as I can be, scout's honor." Kirkpatrick crossed his heart, then felt like a corny asshole as soon as he had. That he couldn't keep his cool was a testament to how long it had been since he'd chatted up a woman this pretty.

"Okay," Officer Meadows said. She started punching some keys into her keyboard.

"Okay what?" Kirkpatrick replied, confused.

"I'm gonna get you your information. If you keep being nice, I might not even tip anyone off that you're around town." She smiled now, and Kirkpatrick realized she'd been putting him on.

"You were just messing with me, huh?"

"Yup."

"And you would have told me what I needed even if I hadn't come clean?"

"Maybe, maybe not. What can I say? Girl has got to do something to make things interesting on the late shift."

Kirkpatrick smiled back and nodded, wondering what she'd done to draw the duty. Maybe she wasn't a team player, but more likely it was good old-fashioned sexism, more alive and well in most small Texas towns than anywhere else he could think of, really. "Is everyone else at this place as much fun as you are?" he asked.

"I doubt it, but it depends on what you consider fun. Your man Watts was picked up on DWI, that's all I can see at the moment. He hasn't finished booking in yet, but that's the only charge pending as of now. He should go before the judge first thing in the morning and be out right after. Does that help you?"

Kirkpatrick shook his head. "Sort of. Can I ask you a kind of personal question?"

"Depends on what you mean by personal."

"You're really into interpretation, aren't you?"

Meadows shrugged, didn't reply.

"I guess I'll take a shot then. What would you say my chances are of notifying the sheriff we're in town without him following us around with a magnifying glass the rest of our time here?"

Meadows looked around to be sure nobody was listening to them, leaned in. "I'd say you've got a better chance of turning water into wine, but that's just my *interpretation*. You'll have to ask everyone else to get theirs." She smiled again, and Kirkpatrick thought she might even be flirting with him a little.

"That's about what I figured."

"Anything else, Ranger Kirkpatrick?" Meadows said.

"Please, call me Russ," Kirkpatrick said.

"Okay, Russ. My name's Evelyn, but most people call me Evie. Round here it's Corporal Meadows, if anyone even speaks to me."

Kirkpatrick thought he had to be reading the signs right, disgruntled cop stuck on the front desk, probably after she had to beat all the hounds away with a stick, which hurt their egos. He decided to take a shot. "Well, Evie, I'm gonna be in town a couple days on this thing, I think. I appreciate you giving me the info and keeping my business on the down low. I could use someone local who might be willing to tell me a little about the ins and outs around here. Any chance you might give me a call if you hear anything else about my man Watts or would you maybe let me know when he gets released?"

Meadows frowned, then seemed to relax it until it almost upended to a smile. She glanced around the room again to confirm they were still alone, beckoned with her finger for him to lean in, and spoke with her lips so close to his ear he could feel the heat from her breath. She said, "We're not really supposed to do that kind of thing, Russ. So I'd be happy to. And don't worry, your secret's safe with me."

Kirkpatrick had to keep himself from shivering. Girl smelled damn good, like sunshine and puppies. He straightened himself, tried to keep it professional. "I really appreciate that," he said as she eased back to her side of the desk. He took out his wallet and passed a business card across the table. "Here's my card. That's my cell there at the bottom. Call me at any hour if you've got something. You always work nights like this?"

Meadows scrunched her face up. "Not always, just haven't been making a lot of friends lately. Moved out here from Dallas with my fiancée, realized he wasn't the one, and here I am, runt of the litter and female, too. Sheriff is on a mission to make sure everyone knows what I can do with my high-falutin' Dallas attitude, too."

"Sounds like the job. Same shit, different department."

"Not the one I signed up for, though." Meadows produced a business card from a drawer in front of her and flipped it over, wrote something on the back, "That's my cell on the back," she said. "I'm on the desk again tomorrow until five a.m., but I've got Sunday off, by some miracle."

"I'll give you a call if something comes up. By the way, got any suggestions on where to get good eats around here?"

"Yeah, lots of them. But you'll have to give me a call if you want to hear about it." They exchanged grins as Kirkpatrick put on his hat and turned to head back out the door.

"When you put it like that, I probably won't eat until I do," he said, then pushed back out the glass doors into the humid night.

CHAPTER FOURTEEN

"Thanks for getting us out," Sancho said to Bobby as they drove back to his lake house around four a.m. "I see y'all got some pull around this place. They're dropping the DWI charge, didn't even check my blood."

Bobby was glad that he was able to do at least that much for his friend. He doubted Sancho would be thanking him for coming to get him if he knew what was coming. This bullshit was exactly why he didn't want Jack Gables and Troy to know about their plan up front. The motherfuckers were both sadists, always had to do things the hardheaded, mean-spirited way. Bobby would have taken another DWI himself if it meant he wasn't gonna have to rip his friend off, or at least the friends of his friend.

Now he would probably never be able to show his face in Austin again, once word got out. Bad enough being the superstar fallen from glory. But the guy who rips his friends off? Son of a bitch.

Sancho slept until noon, but the most Bobby could manage was a couple of restless chunks of half sleep where his conversation with Jack Gables and Troy kept waking him up to repeat itself.

"You said you want in, but it don't sound like you want in," Troy had said when Bobby told them absolutely not, no way he was ripping his homeboy off. He'd pleaded with Troy, tried to explain that this thing could turn into a regular deal, a long-term connection.

Jack Gables had snickered and said, "A bird in the hand is worth two in the bush."

Whatever the fuck that meant. Troy had just smiled, probably relishing the chance to make Bobby screw his friends over. Troy was fucking psycho, and Gables didn't have to make sense, wouldn't have cared if he did. Troy just wanted to see Bobby lose every last bit of dignity he had left.

When he was at UT they'd all been jealous of him, secretly hoping he'd fuck it up, probably knowing he would, actually. Gables was an Aggie, always held it against Bobby that he went to UT. Once Bobby finally did fall out of the tree, they were all pleased as punch to watch him hit his head on every goddamn branch on the way back down. He might be a fuck-up, but how he came from such a long line of sadists, he'd never understand.

"Why do we have to rip them off?" Bobby had asked, still not understanding.

"Because you never pay for what you can take for free," Gables said. "And around here there ain't no one to stop me."

He was right. Bobby had seen that right away. He liked Sancho, but these shitheads couldn't care less about that.

Bobby forced himself to get up around two when he heard Sancho milling around in the kitchen, looking for food, which was a lost cause. Even when he had food, Bobby was prone to eating it all up in a drunken stupor at the end of the night.

"Morning sunshine," Sancho said. "Hungry as fuck, bro. Was looking for some food."

Bobby shrugged as if to say sorry, we don't carry that. "You wanna go ahead and call your guys? Probably wondering what the deal is," Bobby said, honestly just wanting to get this shit over with, now that he knew what it was going to be.

"Let's swing over to El Charito and grab some grub first," Sancho said. "I'm fucking famished. Besides, they're probably sleeping in after the drive. I could really use a couple margaritas."

You're gonna need more than that after tonight, Bobby thought. Goddamnit. Fucked off a multi-million dollar contract and now he couldn't even get in the drug game without jacking something up. He could swear at some point he used to be a winner, but it was long gone now. He'd pleaded with Troy and Gables. He'd tried to focus on the long-term potential, but something inside him felt guilty now, like he should have worked harder to make them see there was more money in the long-term partnership.

They took the Loop over into the older section of town, which had seen better days. Development had shifted south twenty-five years ago, and most of the wealthy white people shifted with it, turning Finney Avenue into a Mason-Dixon line down the middle of town.

Back in high school Bobby used to go to the north side, hunting down ounces of schwag or occasionally some blow or molly, when he got lucky. Troy would have whipped his ass for that, too, but Bobby's father Teddy was still alive back then. Back then he mostly hooked up through his home boy Sheldon, the only black guy he'd ever known to drive a Ninja motorcycle. Oddly enough, Sheldon was the only guy in town who would hook him up now that Troy had put out the word, though he no longer drove the bike.

El Charito was housed in an old ranch-style house that must have been built sometime around 1960. It had a red-and-green neon sign slapped out front facing Fifth Avenue. They parked in the back corner of the lot, behind the hired security guard's old blue F-150, Bobby wanting to keep a low profile, not have to introduce Sancho around to anybody right before he hung the motherfucker out to dry. He'd hoped almost spending a night in the clink would have Sancho keeping a low profile, too, but the guy had always been wild as fuck. Right now he was acting like they'd just got back from the prom or something, raring to party some more.

A blast of AC hit them as they opened the paneled double doors and stepped inside the restaurant. The entry hall opened up into three small dining areas, each probably having at one time been a bedroom or family room, but now with maroon booths lining the walls, like they had for the last thirty years, at least.

A Mexican girl who couldn't have been more than fifteen seated them at one of the booths, and almost before they sat a middle-aged man who probably couldn't speak a word of English brought out a wooden bowl of chips and two syrup containers full of salsa, one the regular house version, the other a special version that was hotter and had chunks of peppers in it.

Bobby had always been partial to the special hot sauce, though his go-to dish had always seemed anything but special. He liked that their bean-and-cheese nachos were baked on house-made tostada shells with so much cheese it would leave long strings attached to the nacho when you tried to bite into it. Bobby preferred to use a knife and fork to eat them, but they were one of his favorite dishes, reminded him of childhood dinners back before his mom ran off with the tennis pro and his dad died from hard living as much as anything else.

Francesca, one of the restaurant's longtime waitresses, came over to get their order.

"Hey, Bobby, twice in one week, huh? Good to see you again," she said, not even getting out her pad, already knowing what Bobby would order.

"Whadaya say, Frannie," Bobby said. "I could, I'd make it every day."

Frannie smiled. "Don't I know it. Who's your friend?"

Sancho started to introduce himself but Bobby cut him off. "This here's Sanch," he said. "Sanch, this is Francesca, but everyone calls her Frannie. She been working here as long as I can remember."

"Howdy," Sancho said.

"Nice to meet you," Frannie replied. "Y'all want something to drink?"

This time Sancho beat him to the punch. "What's y'all's strongest margarita?" he asked.

"I can do you a primo margarita on the rocks, bring out a grandma floater, if that suits your fancy? We can't legally add the floater in a dry county, but I'd imagine you can figure it out."

"Just my style. Bring two," Sancho said. "One for each of us."

Frannie looked Bobby in the eye, and he knew exactly what she was thinking. Troy would beat the shit out of him if he found out he was out drinking in public. He might beat the shit out of her for serving Bobby, for that matter.

Bobby was supposed to be clean and sober or so Troy had decreed around town. Last night had been risky enough, but hanging out at Vernon's, he hadn't been worried about running into anyone, as it was mostly a black's place. He nodded his okay to Frannie, who shrugged and wandered off to the bar area to put in their drink order.

"What was that about?" Sancho asked, noticing the interaction.

"Aw, shit, nothing. She knows my uncle, is all. According to him I ain't supposed to be drinking. Asshole thinks he's my daddy now."

"I'd say fuck him, but I'm thankful he got us out last night. Seems like a pretty good uncle to me, just based on that."

Bobby shrugged now, not really knowing what to say to that, knowing Sancho's opinion of Troy would come clear soon enough. Maybe if they wasted enough time drinking margaritas, Sancho's boys would say fuck it and leave town, save everyone not named Troy Burnell a lot of heartache. Bobby still couldn't sit straight, knowing he was going to rip off his friend.

"How's the carne asada here?" Sancho asked, snapping Bobby back into the moment.

"The wha—oh, it's good. I always get bean and cheese nachos, but really everything on the menu is good."

"So it's really dank or just okay?" Sancho asked, forcing Bobby to interact with him.

"Yeah, it's dank. Believe it or not, the chicken fried steak is just about the best thing on the menu," Bobby said. His father had always been partial to their chicken fried steak, swore you could judge a Tex-Mex restaurant strictly by whether they offered chicken fried steak at all.

The phone rang before he could say anything else, and he looked down to see Troy's number on the screen.

"What's up?" he said as he answered.

"You mean yes, sir, right?" Troy said.

Bobby exhaled, but tried not to do it into the phone. "Yes, sir, sorry. Is there something you need from me?"

"That's better. And yeah, as a matter of fact there is. You need to entertain your friends and keep them on the line until tomorrow. I forgot that I've gotta go over to Shreveport for an unsanctioned fight night, handle the gambling and make sure the fighters get paid. When I get back you better have this thing ready to go or it's your ass. We clear?" Bobby cringed, didn't respond. "Speak up, motherfucker," Troy added.

"Yeah, we're clear," Bobby said.

"Good. I'll call you back at some point, be sure you answer your fucking phone." Troy hung up without saying goodbye, but Bobby was used to that.

"What's up?" Sancho said, apparently reading his face. "Some sort of problem?"

Bobby hesitated, wanted to make sure he made everything sound right. "Nah, everything's good. Except we got to wait until tomorrow now on this thing. My uncle had to go to Shreveport to pick up some money or something, doesn't want me doing business until he gets back. Family policy. When we finish eating let your boys know the deal, they're welcome to stay at my place tonight."

Sancho shrugged. He'd never been that big on keeping to any sort or schedule, far as Bobby could tell.

"Tomorrow, huh? I'm good with that. I doubt they'll like it much, but I don't guess they'll have much choice. I'll invite them out to your place and we can have some fun on the lake. These dudes are a lot of fun, usually, so it'll be all good."

Bobby stopped just short of a shudder, not wanting to have to hang out with the dudes for a day before stealing their shit. "Sure," he said, "I don't see why not." He took a big drink off his margarita, decided to change the subject and bide his time. "So whatcha gonna eat?" he said.

"I think I'ma get the carne asada and have them drop a fried egg on top, live a little."

Bobby figured that was just fine, let him live a little, if he could. For now, Bobby himself was just hoping that some sort of miracle would come along and absolve him of this wretched task.

Maybe he ought to wish someone would pop his uncle Troy over in Shreveport, steal his gambling money and leave him bleeding on the sidewalk. With Troy gone, there'd be nobody in the family left to take charge except Bobby, so long as his uncle Zach was still doing a couple of years of his stretch. Wouldn't that be something. In the end he'd still be stuck with Jack Gables, though. There were some things you couldn't get out of no matter how much you wanted to. Christ, what in the hell had happened to him? It was like that accident killed his future but left his physical body intact to wallow in the mess. This wasn't the way he thought things would turn out at all, and he was getting sick of always having to be the person getting fucked. But what could he do?

CHAPTER FIFTEEN

"Whatcha got for me, Javi?" Kirkpatrick said, still swallowing. "Sorry, just finishing up a little breakfast on a bun."

"You know that shit will kill you, right?"

"I do."

"Anyway, I got a little problem here, my man."

"Shoot."

"I lost Watts and Bobby Burnout. Motherfuckers tore out of the restaurant parking lot so fast you shouldn't be surprised if they end up back in the can for another DWI, since they both had two souped-up margaritas with their lunch. I tried to keep up, earned myself a little fender bender for the trouble. I ever tell you yet how much I love this fucking Camaro?"

"Shit, Javi, I'm sorry to hear it. What happened?"

"It could have been worse. Nobody got hurt. Rear-ended an old lady who stopped short on a yellow light. She was so scared that I'll be lucky if I don't get sued, so if I was y'all, I'd be ready to cover the tab, since I'm on the job."

"I'll take care of you. Any idea where Watts and Burnell headed off to?"

"Not really. Maybe back to Bobby Burnell's place."

"I figured as much."

"If you want, you can come scoop me up after the tow truck gets here and takes my ride away; we can drive around searching. I know the general area where it was, but those coves are confusing."

"I'll come scoop you up, but I don't think it will do much for us to drive around blind."

"How you want to play it, then?"

"I made a bit of a local contact on the down low at the Sheriff's Department last night. Let me give her a call and see if she might point us to the exact address."

"*Her*, huh? Funny how you never make friends with anyone that has a johnson when you visit other departments."

"Not all that funny, really, they smell nicer and smile from time to time, which I like."

"Shit, I know what you like, and it's more than their smell."

"That may be true, but I sure don't get a lot of it these days. Anyway, let me give her a call. Text me the cross streets where you are, I'll be there shortly and we can drop by the motel to get you a change of drawers."

"Very funny. Ten-four," Perez said, hanging up.

Kirkpatrick dug out Meadows's business card and dialed her cell number. It rang four times and went to voicemail. He left a message, reminding her who he was, not that he thought she'd forget, and asking her to give him a call back, if she could.

She was probably asleep after the long night shift, would call him back later. All they could do for now was head back to the motel and maybe try to trace their way back to the house. Weldon Robb was going to try to ruin his career if they let this one fall through, but he was starting to wonder if he still gave a shit about that or if he just wanted to nail this little shit Watts for causing everyone so much trouble. Busting Burnell would bring with it a whole lot of attention he wasn't convinced he wanted, really.

Kirkpatrick drove across town to the intersection Perez texted to him, arrived just in time to see Perez's grey Camaro being loaded up onto a flatbed tow truck and driven away. An ambulance and two police cruisers flanked the tow truck on the shoulder of the road. As Kirkpatrick pulled into the El Charito parking lot, Perez waved him over. He shook hands with a man who must have been one of the tow truck drivers, then moved over to the back of the ambulance, where an elderly woman who looked like she just came out of the beauty salon was still being checked out by paramedics. Perez patted her on the shoulder and said something, but the old woman shot him a nasty look and shook her head. A traffic cop handed Perez what looked to be a ticket. Kirkpatrick was still laughing about the old woman's attitude when Perez opened the passenger door on the truck and climbed inside.

"Oh, you're laughing at me, too, now, KP?" Perez said. Kirkpatrick tried to wipe the smirk off his face, was pretty sure he failed though.

"I was waiting for her to hit you over the head with her purse like a Monty Python skit or something," Kirkpatrick said.

Perez gave his own smirk now. "Man, I don't know what it is. But every time I'm around you and Mexican food, my shit gets all fucked up."

"Sorry about your ride, man. I know I sort of got you wrapped back up in this Weldon Robb shit, but I do appreciate your help. I'll make sure we get the damage covered some way or other."

"She'll never be brand new again, though," Perez said.

"I know it. Anyway, for now let's see what we can do to get back on Watts's trail. I'm waiting on a call on the address. But hopefully we can find out where Bobby Burnout's place is on our own. We'll stop by the motel so you can change your britches, I'm sure you crapped in them when you hammered into that old lady's Buick." Kirkpatrick burst out laughing again, the joke just as good the second time around.

"Yeah, yeah, very funny," Perez said. "Probably ought to just grab my shit and leave you here on your own to deal with these yoyos."

"And miss all the fun?"

"Yeah, some fun," Perez said, shaking his head. "Man, I love that car."

"You know I'm just giving you trouble. You want, when this is all over, I'll take you to my guy Fernando down in Buda, he'll fix you up brand new and sell you some used rims for it, too."

Perez chuckled.

"Now what's so funny?" Kirkpatrick said.

"You think I need me a white boy to know where to come up on some used twenties. Don't let the clothes fool you, I grew up in the barrio back in San Antonio."

"See there, I knew I had you pegged for some sort of ex-cholo."

"Watch it now, Russ. Only gang I was in was the U.S. Marine Corps."

"That's the scariest one."

"Damn straight. Semper fi, motherfucker," Perez said, laughing. "But yeah, roll through the motel, I gotta take a dump real quick. Been pinching it off for hours now, need to lighten my load after that meal."

Kirkpatrick turned right onto the Loop that made a circle around Teller, headed back for the motel. He decided to lay off giving Javi shit for a little while. He knew Javi had done a couple of tours in Fallujah, almost certainly killed some folks, though they'd never swapped stories or compared scars. Kirkpatrick's time in Desert Storm had been much tamer, no doubt. His phone lit up as he was pulling into the motel's parking lot, but he knew without checking it wouldn't be Meadows. It was like Weldon Robb could smell it every single time they had an inch of trouble.

"Kirkpatrick," Kirkpatrick said into the phone, trying to sound busy but professional.

"Mr. Kirkpatrick, tell me some good news. Is Watts shit-canned and sitting in the clink or did y'all fuck it up again?"

"Good to hear from you, Senator," Kirkpatrick started in, wanting to tell the fat asshole a brochure's worth of information about some of the places he could fuck off to. "Had a little bit of a delay, but things are on track overall." It sounded like a lie, even to Kirkpatrick, when he said it, but he'd never been a good liar either way.

"To me that sounds like the first sentence in a series of sentences that end with you telling me y'all screwed the pooch again. Please tell me I'm wrong. It gets hard always having to be right."

"I don't doubt it," Kirkpatrick said, rolling down the window and spitting out of it. "Things have developed a bit since we spoke last, Senator. Watts's contact down here turned out to be somebody you probably know." Kirkpatrick pulled into a spot and parked, motioned for Perez to go on up to the room and get his business done.

"I doubt it," Robb said, frustration rising in his voice now. Kirkpatrick needed to cool off and reel him back in.

"My apologies, Senator, I don't appear to be communicating well today. I meant you've probably heard *of* his contact. It's Bobby Burnell."

There was a pause on the other end of the line, just as Kirkpatrick figured there would be. Weldon Robb was one of the most rabid Texas A&M boosters in the state, hated everything that had anything to do with the University of Texas.

"No shit?" Robb started in. "Bobby Burnout is in the marijuana business? People have always said his family was the closest thing you'd find to scum outside of a stagnant pond."

"I'm not sure about all that just yet, Senator, but he seems involved—"

"Where are they now, do you have your eyes on them?" Robb cut in.

"I—no, Senator, not at the moment. We're about to pick them up again at Burnell's place. Our man Watts got himself picked up on a DWI by the local boys last night. All signs are that the deal is still on, though. I'll keep you updated once I know more." Kirkpatrick braced for the shit storm he knew was about to come through the phone.

"So you aren't with him right now, then, correct, Mr. Kirkpatrick?"

Kirkpatrick sighed, sat back. "No, sir." He watched a couple of shaggy guys as they came down the concrete stairs and walked to the Coke machine right in front of where he was parked. Something was familiar about them, though maybe he'd just seen them last night when he arrived, something like that. Robb's aggressive tone shook him back into the conversation.

"I knew it. Y'all are gonna fuck this deal up. You came well recommended. I have no idea why; so far you ain't been worth a damn on this thing. "

"Senator, I—"

"No, sir, shut your mouth. I'll talk. You listen. I'm so hopped up right now I could shit out a coconut. I absolutely cannot stand Bobby Burnout. That son of a bitch ran all the fuck over our boys when he was at UT. I never seen the Twelfth Man so demoralized in all my seventy years. Knowing he's involved, it changes everything for me. I want that little shit's head on a swivel almost as much as I want Watts's. If you fuck this up there's no telling what I'll do. Am I clear on that, Mr. Kirkpatrick?"

Kirkpatrick didn't answer, focused again on the two shaggy guys as they got drinks out of the machine. He knew them, but how? All at once, it ran over him like a truck. "Senator, I've got to call you back," he said, wanting to just hang up, but not wanting to hear about it from Robb later. Robb started to say something else, but this time Kirkpatrick cut him off. "No really I got to go," he said, really wanting to hang up now.

"Boy, don't you dare hang up on me," Robb said.

"Senator, I'm sitting here looking at our boys from Colorado standing right in front of my truck," Kirkpatrick said. "I'll have to call you back." Weldon Robb shouted something as Kirkpatrick hung up the phone and watched Cooper Daniels and Trevor Davis—both easily recognizeable from the mug shots he'd had faxed over from Dumas—took their sweaty Cokes back up the stairs and inside room 206.

CHAPTER SIXTEEN

Cooper had tried Sancho five times by one p.m., wanting to get out of that hot room ASAP, even though they had it through the next night. They'd walked over to the Whata-burger next door to the motel and had another round of burgers, but Sancho still hadn't called when they got back. Around three o'clock they had to finally say fuck it and head over to the storage place to meet the local CRATES driver, who was delivering their CRATE. Cooper hoped he could slip this guy another fifty to wait around while they emptied it real quick or else swing back by in an hour and pick it back up. He didn't want any trouble with the place's owner, though the man had seemed nice over the phone.

They headed out to the storage unit beneath a tunnel of pine trees on Old Teller Highway, interrupted in spots by fields with oil derricks pumping in them, in others by run-down gas stations or undeveloped tracts of red clay hills with dirt bikes zipping around on them.

"Pretty town," Davis remarked. Cooper agreed, the place was about as clean as anywhere he'd ever been. Back in Conroe everything had always had a shit-tone to it, like even the sidewalks or shopping mall facades had done too much hard living and were paying for it now.

Teller seemed to have a line right down the middle where everything on one end was less than twenty-five years old, and everything on the other had been forgotten for at least thirty. He'd forgotten how racially divided Texas still was compared to Colorado. In all fairness, Colorado had about twenty-five black people, total, who lived outside of Denver, so maybe things there weren't all that much better. Still, a huge portion of Texas seemed to be stuck in the Jim Crow days just as much as anywhere in the Deep South ever was. The southwest had its own brand of racism, too, and it extended as much to Hispanics as it did to blacks. In fact those two groups seemed to refuse to live around each other, as well.

It reminded Cooper how much he didn't want to come back here, didn't want to move to The Woodlands and live in some brick track home that looked just like all the others around it, surrounded by people whose idea of "live and let live" meant they lived and you let them. Too much religion, too money-obsessed. He had to find a way to stay and support his coming family in Colorado.

"You solving the world's problems or what?" Davis said, snapping him out of his head. Davis smiled to show he was joking, added, "Just don't want you to put us in the ditch or something."

"I'm good," Cooper said. "Thinking about Josie, wondering how I'm gonna make money when we get back. Josie wants us to move down here and be closer to her parents. I'd forgotten how much Texas gives me the heebie-jeebies."

Davis nodded, looked back out his window. "It is pretty out here in Teller County, though, gotta admit it. But I'm with ya. I'd sure like to stay right where we're at in Denver. You ever consider maybe getting on with one of the dispensaries, overseeing cultivation or something? I can't imagine there's too many of them who can produce your numbers, all soil organic."

"It crossed my mind. Got no idea what they pay, though. I doubt anyone still gives a fuck if it's organic or not, either."

"Actually, I read in the *Westword* the other day that it's starting to be a trend, boutique connoisseur shops. Kind of exclusive, have to make an appointment, that kind of thing."

Cooper tapped on the wheel, thinking now. "Something to keep in mind, I guess," he said after a little while. "Tell you the truth, I'm just worried Josie won't be there when I get back."

Davis waved the idea away with his left hand. "She'll be there, Coop. Girl loves you, no doubt about it. She'd be as lost without you as you would without her."

"I'm not so sure. She looked pretty upset last time I saw her. Felt like communication had already deteriorated to about nothing."

"She'll cool off. I guess for right now all we can do is keep our heads in the game, get this thing put to bed and hightail it back to safer country."

"Agreed," Cooper said, turning into the storage place. At least the CRATES guy wasn't there yet. It would give him some time to smooth the owner over. Now that the package was due to arrive, his nerves were pumping. Davis seemed cool as a cucumber, but Cooper knew better. They'd both feel a hell of a lot better once it was locked up in the storage unit. Cooper shifted the truck into park and took off his seatbelt. "Be right back," he said to Davis. "Stay put."

The heat and humidity blasted him in the face as he stepped out of the truck. Summer, another thing he'd never missed about Texas. Felt like they'd been born on the sun after living so long in the cool, dry Colorado air.

A bell clanged on the office door when he entered. "Be right out," a man's voice called through the open doorway just behind the counter. White tail deer heads covered the walls at various points, with a few stacks of boxes to the left of the counter and a rack with packing tape and bubble wrap on the other side. Pretty basic local business, far as Cooper could tell. Exactly what he'd been looking for.

"I help ya?" a skinny, balding old man coming out of the back room said, wiping his hands on his stained wranglers. "Sorry, our damn copier is on the fritz again. Was back there trying to tinker it into compliance."

"No problem," Cooper said, laying on the accent. "Long as you don't make me wait outside, I'll wait all day. Good Lord it's hot out there."

"You see now, you got a hundred percent of that right. Anyway, how can I help you?"

"I reserved a unit online the other day. David Schools." Cooper stuck his hand over the counter for a shake.

"Ronald Kidd," the old man said as he returned the handshake. "Let me look through my stuff real quick, I remember making a file on you."

Cooper expected him to step over to the computer, was surprised when instead he opened a drawer below the counter and thumbed through some manila file folders before pulling one out with his fake name on it. Kidd flipped it open to give it a better look.

"Colorado, huh?" he said. "What brings you out to East Texas then?"

"Ah hell, you know," Cooper said, buying some time. "Got a job lined up, wire line crew, most likely."

"Ah, so you must be working for Ambrose Oil, then."

Cooper hesitated, not sure how to answer. "Ambrose, yeah, exactly," he said. "How'd you know?"

"Ambrose is about the only one operating in the county. My boys went to school with Tim Ambrose. Guy's sharp as a tack. You meet him face to face, tell him ol' Ronnie Kidd says to take care of you, and he'll do ya."

"I'll keep it in mind," Cooper said.

"Anyhow, five-by-seven unit for one month, correct?"

"That's right."

"Just need to see some ID and a credit card."

"Yeah, about that. See, I'm planning to pay cash. Truth is I just got divorced, had to nix all the credit cards as part of that, woman kind of burned things down in terms of my credit, if you get me."

Ronald Kidd frowned. "You paid online. Card's for deposit," he said. "In case you stay longer or tear something up and don't want to pay." Cooper started to try to explain again, but Kidd cut him off. "However, I done been through a divorce or two myself now, so it's your lucky day. First thing they go for is the credit, like a dog on a bone. Tell you what. Put up an additional month as a deposit, we'll call it good. Keep in mind I know your boss, so don't do nothing squirrelly, make me feel foolish."

"You got my word on it. I appreciate your candor. Been pretty rough as of recent," Cooper said, channeling his very real fear of losing Josie into his face. "Part of the reason I moved."

"You from Teller?" Kidd asked.

"Nah, down Conroe way. But a job's a job, so here I am." Cooper wished he hadn't mentioned where he was really from, but it was too late.

"Huh. Lived down there with my first wife." Kidd leaned in close, and added, "Too many niggers down there for my taste. Least they stay where they belong round here."

Cooper focused on controlling the look on his face. He didn't need any waves right now, just wanted to get out and get the CRATE unloaded. "I hear ya," he finally managed, then changed the subject. "So listen. I've got CRATES dropping off a mobile storage unit of my stuff for me. Apartment won't be ready for a couple weeks as it turns out so I'm in a hotel, and CRATES storage fees are too damn high, I just want to be rid of them. Thought I would be moving right into my place when I hired them. Anyway, I'm gonna get the driver to pick it right back up in an hour or so, just wanted to see it was all right with you if it sits there for an hour or so."

Kidd scrunched his face up at the word CRATES. "You ask me, they too damn high all around. I always counsel folks away from them. Moving company and storage is cheaper. They trying to run all the local boys out of the game. That said, I appreciate you doing business with me. Long as they have their asses back off my property within two hours, I'll look the other way. Fair?"

"Fair enough," Cooper said. "I appreciate you being so courteous on everything."

"You're back in Texas now, son. It's how we do things."

Cooper nodded. He filled out some more documents and tried to avoid chatting any further. Kidd didn't seem taken aback by his ID, handed it back like it was any other.

Kidd led him outside and across the lot to a small unit off the backside. The CRATES driver was pulled up to the curb, looked like he was about to get out and come over. Cooper pretended not to see him and followed Kidd to the unit.

"Okay, that's pretty much it, unit 192. Use your own lock, but I'd advise you to get a good one. Had a break-in or two before, but only on units that don't use a disk lock. I got 'em for sale back at the counter if you need, nineteen-ninety-five apiece. You don't get out or don't pay on time, you forfeit the deposit, and I'll put a lock on the unit until you settle up the additional charges. Got it?"

"Straight," Cooper said, just wanting to get rid of the

man now. "Got my own disk lock. I sure appreciate you helping me out."

"No problem." Kidd glanced up as the CRATES guy approached. "Just be sure this jerk has his contraption back out of here before closing. And don't block the driveway." Kidd turned and wandered back across the boiling asphalt to the office.

"What's he talking about?" The CRATES guy said by way of greeting. "We don't do same-day pickup. You're Mr. Schools, right?"

"I am. Unfortunately there's been a change of plans," Cooper lied. Guy tells me I got to have the CRATE off his property tonight, no choice. Any way you can come back and get it in an hour?"

"No can do," the driver said, agitation registering on his face. "Got a strict schedule, have to follow it to the letter if I want to get off on time."

Cooper frowned. "Any way I could slip you a fifty to hang back over there in the truck for twenty minutes, then pick this sucker back up and take it with you?"

"I'd rather not, no. Soon as I get back to the yard they'll load me up with another that has to go out at a specific time. If I spend more than twenty minutes here it will start throwing everything into chaos."

Cooper stopped, looked the man in the eye. "Would you rather have that grumpy old man who just walked off take this thing apart with a chainsaw? I get the feeling he ain't accustomed to not getting his way."

"We could drop it off at a separate location for you, or on another day, but that's about it."

"How 'bout this. Back that sucker up to my unit here, my homeboy and I will unload it in twenty minutes without you even taking it off the truck." Cooper took a five-dollar bill out of his pocket, gestured at the Conoco across the street. "Meantime, you hit that store over yonder and grab something cold to drink, my treat, and we'll have you out of here in twenty minutes, no problem, a *hundred* extra bucks in your pocket, too." Cooper added two fifties to the five, extended the money to him.

The driver scratched his stubbled chin. After a moment he took the money and turned to go back to his truck. "Twenty minutes," he said over his shoulder. "I catch heat, I'm telling my boss you threatened to destroy it if I left it."

"That's not quite accurate, but I got you. How 'bout we call it nineteen minutes," Cooper said, knowing they were about to have to bust ass to get it done in that time.

"So be it."

The driver climbed back up in the customized CRATES delivery truck. The truck beeped as he put it in reverse and backed it up in front of the unit. Cooper had sweat running down his ass crack now. Felt like they were hanging out in an oven, standing there on the asphalt. He motioned to the truck. Davis leaned across the seat, killed the engine, and got out.

"What's the deal?" he said as he made his way over, looking miserable in the direct sunlight.

"Sorry to tell you, bubba," Cooper said. "But all's we got is twenty to get this thing unloaded."

"Nineteen," the driver called out, stepping down from the truck and heading toward the Conoco. "Best unlock it and get moving."

CHAPTER SEVENTEEN

When the CRATES truck showed up at the storage place, Kirkpatrick and Perez exchanged an incredulous look, both still sitting in Kirkpatrick's truck, parked at the gas station across the street.

"How much you wanna bet they shipped the dope down in that container?" Kirkpatrick said.

"I'd have to be dumb and stone-blind to think otherwise. Between you and me, I'm impressed. Never seen that before." Perez ran his hand through the sweaty short hair on his head, then wiped the sweat on his jeans.

"Me either. Definitely one to add to the notes." As Kirkpatrick said it he was already writing in his notebook.

"So what do you think, do we hymn them up now, or wait?"

Kirkpatrick shook his head. "Let's wait. I got a feeling they're gonna stash it away in that storage unit, but if not, we'll box them in when the time comes. Maybe at the motel."

"You think they'll roll over on their people?"

"I don't know, maybe. I don't imagine they'll be too keen on the alternative. Far as I'm concerned, my only mandate right now is putting the chains on Elroy Watts and Bobby Burnell. Senator Robb has as big of a hard-on for Bobby Burnout as he does Watts, now."

Perez nodded, appeared to think that over. "Redneck

geezer probably loves his Aggies at least as much as he does his grandson I could see that."

Kirkpatrick rolled down the windows and shut off the engine. They sat like that, heat bearing down, for a couple of minutes, until Cooper Daniels handed the driver what looked like some money, and the driver turned and headed across the street toward them. They both tensed up when the driver passed by Kirkpatrick's window so close that Kirkpatrick could have reached out and touched him, though the driver didn't pay them any mind.

"You want me to go in and check out the driver, see if I can chat him up?" Perez said. "You know, in case he's involved?"

"You read my mind. Just be quick in case our boys get back on the move. Guy's probably taking a piss or something. My assumption is they're paying him to break some kind of protocol."

"Shit, he's getting something cold to drink, guaranteed. Only reason I suggested I go inside is I want something cold for myself." Perez opened the door and got out. He closed it and stuck his head back through the window. "Want anything?"

"A Coke would be nice. In a can, if you don't mind. Thanks, Javi."

"Thanks nothing," Perez said, hand in through the window now. "You're paying."

Kirkpatrick snickered and pulled out his wallet, tossed a couple of bills on the seat so that Perez had to lean in farther to pick them up.

"Real nice touch," Perez said, heading off toward the convenience store's glass doors.

Kirkpatrick turned the key enough to let the radio play, scanned through the stations but couldn't find anything worth hearing, so he shut the key back off and settled in for a good sweat. Across the street, Daniels and Davis were unloading what looked to be a load of ratty furniture into the storage unit. Probably had the dope hidden in the couch or something. Least that's where Kirkpatrick would have hidden it, had he been a drug-smuggling half-hippy itching to find his way to state prison.

Before long both men's shirts were soaked through with sweat. They were gonna be even hotter down in Huntsville. The thought of that alone ought to be enough to make them ready to cooperate. Kirkpatrick wasn't far behind in the sweat department, was thinking about rolling up the windows and cranking the AC when Perez climbed back into the truck, a sweating can of Coke in one hand and an orange Gatorade in the other.

"Find anything out?" Kirkpatrick said.

"Not really. Guy's kind of a prick. Lot of that going around lately. I think he's letting them unload the container without dropping it off, probably slipped him some money to do it like you said, but he didn't say that."

"Makes sense." Kirkpatrick started to say something else, but shut up when the driver passed by his window again, this time headed back to the storage lot. It looked like the suspects had finished unloading the container.

"You see them unload anything suspicious?" Perez said.

"Yeah. All of it. But I think the dope's probably in the couch. Let's see if they move it after ol' boy takes off."

CHAPTER EIGHTEEN

Cooper was sprawled out from the heat, lying with his head as close to the room's crappy window unit as he could get, when his phone lit up with Sancho's number. Davis sat straight up as Cooper answered the call.

"Sancho, that you man?" he said.

"Wussup, Coop, y'all make it down all good?"

"We did. Just hanging back at the motel, for now. I been trying to call you all day, figured I'd have heard from you either last night or this morning. Everything good?"

"Everything's great, my man. Got a little hung up is all, but everything's been taken care of. So listen. My man's people are out of town until tomorrow, so it looks like we're gonna be a little delayed, nothing I can do. Why don't y'all meet me out at my homeboy's lake house, we've got some girls on the way and a whole truckload of booze, gonna take out the boat and do some wakeboarding, cruise around on some jet skis, that kind of thing. Y'all can stay the night, no problem."

Davis gave Cooper a concerned look that said he could hear Sancho through the phone. Cooper muted his phone, said, "He says the thing is delayed now until tomorrow. Wants us to come out to the lake and hang out, stay the night at his buddy's place. How you wanna play it?"

Davis wiped the sweat off his forehead with his palm. "I don't know, but it's hotter than hell in this shit-box room. I guess maybe we ought to go out there and figure out what the hell's going on."

"That's what I was thinking. Let's play it cool on the booze though, sound good?"

"Coop, you there?" Sancho said. Cooper unmuted the phone.

"Yeah, man, I'm here. Let me grab a pen and I'll write down the address."

"Sound's good," Sancho said. "Just wait about a half-hour to head this way, we're on our way out to the county line to grab some supplies."

"Supplies?" Cooper asked.

"Booze, my friend. Teller County is dry, if you hadn't noticed."

Cooper hadn't. In fact, he hadn't planned on being here long enough to give a damn. He wrote down the address and told Sancho they'd be there in a while, hung up.

"I got a bad feeling about this," Davis said.

"Brother, I ain't feeling too great about it myself. Honestly, I'm more worried about what a day of sitting in that hot storage unit will do to the product than anything else about it. With humidity like this, I wouldn't be surprised to cut the bags open and everything be damp. Might flatten the smell at the very least, flub the whole crop. I ain't about to risk moving it until we see what the deal is, though."

"It'll be okay. I got a couple days behind on trimming at my place, so my part's a little crispy. That fucking Red Rocks Panic run flattened me."

"Let's just hope it doesn't cook off too much of the potency. I grabbed the mini stash so they can check out the product in the meantime. Grab a shower so we can head that way."

* * *

112

They drove out Old Teller Highway beneath a tunnel of pine trees that gave way here and there to rolling pastures, some of them with oil derricks pumping away. It took about fifteen minutes to make it to the northern coves of Lake Strongbow, which looked to be a few feet low. The water only came up to a few feet below the bottoms of the boat-houses that lined each cove's shores.

It still made Cooper nervous, leaving the stash in that storage unit, but he didn't see any way around it. He just didn't trust Sancho enough to go ahead and bring it out to his boy's place. The heavy sun felt like a spotlight even through the truck's tinted windows, made Cooper feel a little bit like they were out on tour, getting in some lake time between shows or something. He'd feel a lot better if Josie would at least answer her phone and give him some sort of reckoning about what was going to happen between them. He loved her, certainly didn't want to lose her. The sooner they could get through this thing and he could get back up there to make things right with her, the better he'd feel.

"It's pretty here," Davis said, nodding his head to the radio and looking out the passenger window. "Everything else aside, I could sure use a dip in that lake. You forget how hot it gets down here, you know?"

"I was just thinking the same thing," Cooper said. "Can't even look out the window without breaking a sweat."

"You doing all right, man? I saw you been nervous as hell all day long. Josie not taking your calls?"

Cooper squeezed the wheel, knowing Davis was trying to help, but not wanting to get into it all when he wasn't even sure what he was feeling himself. "Not yet," is all he said.

Davis seemed to take the hint and went back to looking out the window.

"Coop?" Davis said after another minute.

"Yeah?"

"Everything's gonna be all good, just try not to worry too much. It's a pretty day. For now the stash is out of sight, out of mind, and for all his faults, Sancho can be a lot of fun. Let's see if we can't find a way to enjoy ourselves until tomorrow, worry about the deal then. Sound good?"

"I can dig it," Cooper said, knowing full well that they were both wishful thinking. Davis was just trying to make him feel better, was himself a notorious worrier. But he was right, a couple of cold beers and some good food couldn't hurt anything, so long as they kept a low profile. For Sancho, keeping a low profile would be damn near impossible, but maybe they could manage him enough to get through things and get back home safely. It was a big maybe, but for now it was the only one they had.

The address Sancho had given led them to a long, one-story brick house painted an opaque grey color, set back off the curvy blacktop road that wound through that particular cove of Lake Strongbow.

Cooper pulled the truck down the driveway and parked under a clear plastic basketball goal. A grass hill sloped down to the lake's shore beyond the house, where a boat-house painted the same color as the main house stuck out into the water. The boathouse had a big open dock on one side along with an iron spiral staircase that led to a deck on the dock's second level that had lounge chairs for sunbathing, and bikini-clad girls lounging in two of them. Out on the cove two jet skis whipped around and appeared to be chasing each other. Cooper could tell right away one of them was Sancho by his froed-out curly hair and tall, lanky frame, which made his life jacket look both too big and too small. His long, pasty white arms didn't look like they'd spent the last six months in Costa Rica.

Cooper parked and he and Davis got out of the truck. The house itself had a big deck off the back, shaded by two giant pine trees that had to be at least fifty years old. The back end of the deck had an iron pit smoker built into it. Cooper's mouth watered at the thought of some Texas barbeque. Maybe they could go grab a bite somewhere later on, since they were stuck in town anyway.

They walked down the stone path to the boathouse as small waves from the jet skis rolled into the cove. Once they walked out onto the pier Sancho seemed to see them, because his jet ski banked and pointed toward the boathouse. Cooper and Davis waved almost in tandem. Slight footsteps moved across the upper deck above them, and a pair of muscular olive legs came down the spiral stairs to reveal a petite brunette in a string bikini colored up like a Texas flag. She held an empty Lone Star bottle by the neck like a club.

Davis straightened up and looked nervous, like he always did around pretty girls. Cooper saluted her with the tip of his Dickies trucker cap and said, "Howdy."

"Howdy, yourself," the girl said. "Who are y'all?"

"We're friends of Sancho, he gave us directions out here. I'm Cooper, and this here's Trevor, but everybody calls him Davis. What's everyone call you?"

The girl tipped down her aviator sunglasses, gave Cooper a look that seemed to ask if he was for real, then noticed Davis checking her out and rolled her eyes at him. "I'm Claire. We're friends of Bobby's, just met your friend Sancho."

"Pleased to meet you, Claire," Davis said. Cooper had to suppress a laugh. Davis was the best guy he knew, but no one was more awkward around a pretty girl, especially a well-endowed one in a loud swimsuit.

"Likewise," Cooper added. "Who's we?"

Claire motioned back up the stairs. "Me and my girl Candace. She's still laying out. I was getting another beer. Y'all want something to drink?"

Cooper hesitated, but Davis was already nodding his head yes and following Claire into the boathouse's storage closet, which had a refrigerator and some racks with kneeboards, wakeboards and skis on them. The boathouse itself housed a black Supra ski boat with a giant chrome rack, over which Cooper and Davis exchanged an impressed look. They'd spent a summer rolling up to Horsetooth Reservoir with Small Paul back when he owned a boat, and Davis had gotten damn good at wakeboarding.

"Maybe we'll get to give it a try here in a few," Cooper said, already knowing what Davis was thinking.

"Maybe? I'm not setting foot off this pier until I do," Davis smiled at Claire as she handed them each a sweaty Lone Star.

"I ain't had a Lone Star in a long time," Cooper said.

"Why not?" Claire asked. "They carry it at almost every bar in town."

"We don't live in town," Davis said.

"Oh yeah?" Footsteps came down the stairs behind Cooper. Outside the boathouse, the jet ski's engines both wound down, meaning Sancho and his friend must be pulling up to the dock. Cooper came back out of the dark boathouse to see Sancho's curly brown mop and oversize designer sunglasses.

"Coop, y'all made it," Sancho called out as he grabbed the pole and pulled the jet ski to the dock, then tied it off with a nylon loop attached there for that purpose. "Whadaya say there, Davis," Sancho added. "Long time no see, brotha."

Sancho came across the dock and pulled Cooper in for the standard half-hug, two dabs on the back. As they did,

Cooper froze when he looked past Sancho and saw Sancho's friend's face.

"No shit?" Cooper asked him, gesturing with his head at Bobby Burnell.

"Fellas, I believe y'all may have heard of Bobby Bigtime?" Sancho grinned from ear to ear. Cooper started to say something but couldn't decide what, so he didn't. Instead he and Davis exchanged a look that said no way you could make this stuff up.

CHAPTER NINETEEN

Bobby winced a little when Sancho called him Bobby Big-time. He hated it when people used that name now, knowing how everything had turned out. He wanted to say something every single time someone used it, but his pride wouldn't allow him to let them see it bothered him that much. It surprised him that he still had any pride left to lose, but not for long now, anyway.

He shook hands with Sancho's two guys, the shaggy-haired one in aviator sunglasses and a Dickie's hat, Cooper, was medium height, a touch athletic looking, though not on Bobby's level, for sure. Looking like exactly what Sancho had said he was, half hippy half country boy in his pearl snap with rolled-up sleeves, dingy Levis jeans and flip flops. He could tell Claire already had her eye on him, which normally would have made him mad, but just now he figured that even if she did give the guy a little ass, it would be the least Bobby could do to stay out of the way, considering the guy was about to come up thirty thousand short tomorrow. Claire had slept with most of his friends by this point anyway.

"Man, I used to watch you play all the time at UT," said Davis, the taller, thinner one in shorts and a T-shirt that read *I'd rather be Driving > Disco.* "When you ran the botched snap in for a touchdown at the end of the Rose Bowl, I screamed myself hoarse. Not there in person, you understand, but we was watching on television. It's damn good to meet you."

"It's good to meet you boys, too," Bobby said, lying, a little miffed that these guys he was gonna have to fuck over were treating him like everybody used to back before his accident. "I could use me a beer," he said, trying to keep things moving forward. It was gonna be a long twenty-four hours and that was a shame.

Leave it to Troy to put him off. Fucker with his ego hard-on about putting on MMA fights. Troy had been an amateur kickboxer fifteen years ago and still acted like he could kick everyone's ass all the time. They could have a pretty nice little party out here under different circumstances, but fucking Troy's shadow loomed over the whole thing now.

"This is your place then, Bobby?" Cooper said.

Bobby hesitated. "Sort of," he said, not wanting to have to explain that it was his family's place, how his uncle might like to torture him the rest of the time, but was nice enough to let him stay here. The house he'd grown up in had been sold after his father died, and like all of their assets belonged to the family's trust. Troy was the trustee, and Troy trusted Bobby about as far as he could throw him, which was admittedly pretty fucking far, though that wasn't the point.

"Y'all have a good drive down and everything?" Sancho asked.

Cooper took a drink of his beer, nodded. "Nothing to it but the first half of Panic's summer tour on the iPod and a couple double Whataburgers with cheese."

"I always missed the food down here when I lived in Denver," Sancho said. "How's the Panic been lately, anyway? I managed to download one show, but mostly I been out of the loop the last few months."

Davis cut in, "I think it's been one of their best runs in a long time. They been on fire lately. Jimmy Herring is a fucking animal, dude has been shredding everything he touches."

"Shit, he won't never replace Mikie, period," Sancho said. "That's why I ain't even felt too bad about being away. Band ain't what it used to be."

"Maybe not," Cooper said, "but they sure been fooling me."

Sancho laughed and held out his beer in a cheers. Bobby understood they were talking about music, but not much else about the conversation, and he could tell Claire was getting bored with it, too. Maybe he'd get his dick wet tonight after all. Cooper, Davis and Sancho clinked bottles together and took a drink as Candace made her way down the stairs.

Candace was skinnier than Claire, with smaller breasts and a much paler complexion. She looked a little lanky, almost like an awkward teenage girl who hadn't grown all the way up yet. She'd looked even more awkward back in high school, but she'd always given him just a touch of the sex eyes, and though he hadn't ever done anything with her and she wasn't all that much to look at, he'd always vaguely wanted to fuck her for reasons that escaped him. Even now, thinking about it gave him a little bit of a chubby.

"Cooper, Davis, this here's Candace," Bobby said. "Nice to meet you," Candace said, smiling at Davis and then turning to Bobby. "Mind if I get another beer, Bobby?" she added.

"You make yourself right at home, sugar," he replied. "Help yourself to whatever you want." Especially my dick, he thought. He'd always had a weakness for women. No matter how much trouble it got him in, how many times he'd woken up to girls he didn't know, who didn't know how they'd gotten there, and all the anxiety of accusations that came with that, he still couldn't keep it in his pants.

"So I don't think I mentioned it before, but Davis here is a closet wakeboarding professional," Cooper said. "Boy can do all kinds of spins and grabbing around on the board and all that mess."

Davis shrugged. "It's all the snowboarding, seems to carry over pretty well."

Sancho laughed and Bobby nodded as Davis shoved Cooper playfully and mumbled something else about not being all that great, Bobby knowing the whole time he would show any of them up either way. He'd grown up on this lake, had been wakeboarding almost since wakeboards were invented.

If he hadn't been so good at football he might have gone pro. Maybe he still could, he thought, then shook that off right away. The sport had progressed past him in the time he'd been away from it, and even though he didn't need all his fingers to hold on to the rope, something told him he'd be hopelessly behind now.

Besides, it would just be something else for people to give him shit about. He was done giving a damn what the world thought, time to start doing for himself, especially if Troy was gonna make him rip off his friends.

"Tell y'all what," Bobby said, looking forward to the chance to show off a little in front of the girls, who had seen it all before anyway. "Y'all get your swim trunks on and let's hit the lake. I ain't been out in a while myself, could use a little time on the old HyperLite."

"Thing is," Davis said, "I didn't bring any shorts. You, Coop?"

"Sure didn't."

"Couple of knuckleheads," Sancho said. "I thought y'all grew up in Beaumont? How you gonna come to Texas in the summer and not bring shorts?"

Davis shrugged. Cooper said, "Conroe, actually. Guess I forgot."

"I'm sure Bobby's got some y'all can borrow," Sancho said.

Bobby frowned. No way he wanted to get this up close and personal with these guys, but he didn't have much choice. "Yeah, uh, sure I do," he said. "Y'all follow me up to the house and I'll get you fixed up." Bobby pushed past Claire, his shoulder brushing against her tit and making him a little hard. He wished he had some way to signal her to come up with him, might could catch a quick blowjob or something in the bathroom. Instead he gestured for Cooper and Davis to follow him, realized Sancho was gonna come, too, as they headed in a line up the dock and back toward the house.

CHAPTER TWENTY

Kirkpatrick and Perez parked the truck down the road at the entrance to the cove that Bobby Burnell's lake house was in, Perez muttering the whole way that he'd never have found the place again on his own. The black Chevy Suburban in Burnell's driveway had a "Hook 'em Horns" sticker on the back window. Kirkpatrick didn't get a look at Bobby like he'd wanted, having had to drive by a littler faster than he would have liked to avoid spooking anyone.

"Why don't we just park under those nice shade trees over there?" Perez had said when Kirkpatrick pulled around to park, gesturing to an empty Rose Meadows church retreat center parking lot. "It's too hot to be sitting in this truck with the engine shut off in direct sunlight."

"You ever spend much time out of San Antonio or Austin, living in a small town?" Kirkpatrick asked him. "Maybe in college, something?"

"Nah, not really. Went to school at San Antonio College. Why?"

"That's what I figured. In small towns there's no more avid a defender of private property rights than a church. Someone would be up in our business in fifteen minutes if we parked over there, guaranteed."

"Don't look like there's anybody there, to me," Perez said. "Besides, we're cops. They'd probably let us stay."

"'Round here gossip probably spreads faster than the

clap. Even if they let us stay, there's a good chance someone we don't want to know we're here might find out."

Perez had just shrugged it off, mumbled something
about Kirkpatrick being paranoid, just wanting to watch
him sweat. But sure enough, within fifteen minutes a man
in khaki shorts with a tucked in white polo shirt came out
of the center's gate and started emptying the trash bags out
of the trashcans at one end of the lot. The man eyed them
as if they'd stolen something out of the cans. Kirkpatrick
grinned and nudged Perez to make sure he saw the guy
looking at them. The issue was dropped after that.

They'd been sitting like that for almost three hours, Kirkpatrick wishing he'd brought some water along, when the
black Suburban came up the road, rock and roll blaring from
the down windows and Bobby Burnell in the driver's seat
with Sancho Watts next to him. None of them seemed to
notice the truck, but Kirkpatrick gave it a good twenty-five
seconds before pulling out on the road and tailing them from
a distance all the way into town, then across Finney Avenue
into the worn-down section of town that surrounded the
downtown square.

They pulled up to the valet lane in front of a place on the
square called Jackson's. The streets downtown were made
from red brick and had to be at least a century old. Kirkpatrick parked half a block down, where he had a good view
of the front of the place. A valet with a slight beard dressed
in a black uniform took the keys from Burnell as Cooper
Daniels and Trevor Davis climbed out of the back along
with a couple of dolled-up girls in fancy sundresses and cowboy boots. Perez whistled at the sight of them. Kirkpatrick
had always liked that look, boots on tan legs with a skirt,
but something about the way these girls wore it made them
look promiscuous. Burnell had always had a thing for fast
women, or so Kirkpatrick had heard. Watts took whatever

he could get, he knew that for a fact.

The group disappeared into the bar as Kirkpatrick and Perez settled in for another hour of the waiting game. Kirkpatrick was just thinking about trying to call Meadows again when, lo and behold, she came walking up the sidewalk and went into the bar, too.

"What are the odds?" Kirkpatrick said out loud.

"What odds?" Perez asked, adding, "Odds of a pretty girl walking in that place? Pretty damn good, from what I've seen."

"Stay here and make sure they don't come back out," Kirkpatrick said, already opening the truck door.

"What? You're going in now on account of a pretty girl? Our guys are in there. What if they see you?"

"They've never seen me before either way, so doesn't matter. Besides, that there's more than a pretty girl. That's my inside man at the Sheriff's Department, Officer Meadows."

Perez grinned and shook his head as Kirkpatrick took his hat off the dashboard and got out. Perez leaned across the bench and said, "I see what you saw in her. When you coming back?"

"I'll be back in a few. If they leave while I'm in there, just stay on them. I'll catch up with you down the road."

Kirkpatrick shut the door and started to walk off, then stopped and turned around. "Here's the keys," he said, tossing them on the bench seat through the window.

"Yeah, yeah," Perez replied," Just try to keep it in your pants. I'm running the AC, by the way."

Kirkpatrick crossed the street and went into the bar. The place was dark inside, with original brick walls down one side and stained concrete floors. A long wooden bar ran across the left side of the place, then beyond that a hallway to the bathrooms, and across from the bar a door out onto the porch, which occupied a space between buildings that had to have been a building itself at one time or another.

He scanned the room but didn't see Meadows, so he went to the bar and ordered a bourbon on the rocks. He dropped a ten and a couple of ones on the bar, then turned to lean his back on it while he casually scanned the room for Meadows. It didn't take long to figure out she wasn't in there, so she had to be on the porch. He pushed through the glass door that led outside and was greeted by a wave of moisture from a series of misters that hung at various spots above the porch. He was on the porch's upper level, which was lined in wrought iron railing and wrapped around a rectangular lower level in the center, which could be accessed by a set of stairs toward the front of the building.

The stage at the back end of the porch had a twenty-something guy in Wranglers, fancy leather boots and a short-sleeve plaid pearl-snap, crooning an old Brooks and Dunn song that Kirkpatrick couldn't remember the name of. Guy had a pretty good voice, actually.

Meadows was seated by herself at a small round table for two with what looked to be a martini in front of her. She looked damn good out of uniform, her bob haircut coming off more stylish but still not wearing much makeup, naturally beautiful in a hometown sort of way. Kirkpatrick liked that she didn't try to cover up her freckles. He found freckles cute as hell.

He made it half way down the stairs before she spotted him. Her eyes narrowed and her face tightened as she looked around the room, almost as if she expected someone to be watching them. The look was so serious that Kirkpatrick looked around, too, but didn't stop coming over.

"Fancy meeting you here," he said, sitting down across from her. Meadows nodded and kept looking over his shoulder. "Am I interrupting something?" Kirkpatrick asked.

Meadows sighed. "No, I don't guess so. You following

your man mighty close, huh? Just saw him and Bobby Burnell and some others inside."

"Yeah?" Kirkpatrick said. "You see where they went to? I couldn't find them. But honestly, I came in here to see you."

"They're upstairs in the private room. They got a couple pool tables up there and the owner lets VIPs hang out, sends a server up to deal with their drinks, I think. Chuck Colston owns the place."

"That supposed to be someone I know?"

"Not really. He's the mayor's brother. This town has a good ol' boy network like you wouldn't believe." Meadows took a sip of her drink, so Kirkpatrick mirrored her and took a sip of his own. "Speaking of good ol' boys, you're sort of cramping my style, Mr. Kirkpatrick."

"Didn't I mention you could call me Russ?"

"You did, and I told you to call me Evie. I'm supposed to have a blind date showing up any minute."

"I think I might call you Meadows, actually. Fits something in your spunky attitude. Blind date?"

"Don't give me that cop eye stuff, Russ," Meadows said. "I see you judging." She gave him a playful kick under the table, but still looked a little uncomfortable. "A girl's gotta do what she's gotta do, and I'm new in town. I know you'll have a hard time believing it, but meeting men isn't exactly easy on the job."

"I have a hard time believing anyone up there can take their eyes off of you to get any work done," Kirkpatrick said. That seemed to do it. A smile slipped out before she could straighten back up, and a hint of red flushed across her face.

"You better quit flirting with me and get going before my date shows up to defend my honor," she said. "He's supposed to be a damn good attorney."

"Well, that settles it, then."

Meadows kicked him again. "Settles what?" she said, traces of a giggle in her tone.

"I can't in good conscience let you sit here by yourself and brave the company of a lawyer. I think the best course of action is for me to be your blind date. I've been told I'm damn fine company at cocktail parties."

Meadows laughed now. "Yeah? I just bet you are. All right, I'll make you a deal then."

"Shoot."

"You can stay, but you're the one who has to tell him he can't. That's him right over there now, actually," she said. Kirkpatrick followed her gaze to a short, greying man in starched Wranglers with snakeskin boots and a grey suit coat with brown patches at the elbows. He looked just like the son of a bitch Melissa had run off and married.

"Done," was all he said, his mouth almost watering at the opportunity.

Meadows sat back with an amused look on her face. The man stopped about ten feet from the table, confused by Kirkpatrick's presence. Kirkpatrick smiled a big smile and waved him over, standing to greet him.

"Well, hey there, sport," he called out as the man inched toward them, obviously not liking how his date was starting off.

"His name is Tom," Meadows said, then added, "I think."

"Well shit, Tom, that's great. Tom, I'm Russ Kirkpatrick. I believe you've met my little sister Courtney here, am I right?"

"I thought your name was Ev—"

Kirkpatrick cut him off. "Nah, it's Courtney. She's sweet, but she's got some mischief in her. Especially since the diagnosis. She forgets to take her meds there's no telling what she'll say."

Meadows snickered, then covered her mouth. She

kicked Kirkpatrick for real under the table this time.

"Ouch," he said, gesturing to her. "See what I mean?"

"What diagnosis?" Tom asked, still standing there, looking even more confused as the musician on stage moved into a rendition of "Ramblin' Man."

"I'm afraid she's got DID. Sounds like you met Evie, though. She's one of my favorites. Much more reasonable than Rambo Bill."

"Rambo Bill?" Tom said. Meadows erupted into laughter, unable to keep it in any longer. Kirkpatrick scooted toward her and put his hand on her shoulder, gave Tom a very serious look. "See what I mean?" he said. "I hate to say it, but I know what you're thinking. 'Batshit crazy,' am I right?"

"I—"

"No need to say anything, Tom. And honestly, brother, I'm really sorry about all the trouble. If Evie was a real person, I think y'all would make a fine couple. But honestly, Evie is Rambo Bill's girl, anyway, so you can probably imagine they're gonna be tearing shit up the rest of the night over this as it is. I'd hate to see you caught up in the middle of it."

"But I thought you said they weren't—"

"Real? Depends on your definition. Anyway, you'd best run along, Tom, before things start getting sketchy. You see that?" Kirkpatrick gestured toward Meadows's face, and to his surprise, she played along, gave Tom an aggressive look. "I think Rambo Bill just got home. Best get while the gettin's good. Hell, I might ought to leave myself." Kirkpatrick stepped back from Meadows and Tom stumbled backward away from the table. Kirkpatrick tipped his hat and winked. Tom sneered at him, but turned and walked back up the stairs where he had come from. Kirkpatrick sat back down.

"How'd I do?" he asked.

Meadows tried to hide her smile by taking a drink, but Kirkpatrick winked to let her know he saw it. She laughed and put her face in her hands, then looked up and met his eyes. "About as good as I've ever seen, actually," she said.

"I'll cheers to that then," Kirkpatrick said, tilting his glass to meet the rim of her martini. She tapped his glass back and took a drink.

Kirkpatrick leaned back in his chair, balanced his drink on his thigh. "Now that that's taken care of, why don't you tell me a little bit about Bobby Burnell, and how our boys managed to get out of jail without seeing a judge last night."

Meadows looked around, like she'd done back at the station when Kirkpatrick first met her. "I don't think we should talk here," she said, leaning in close, forcing him to lean back forward so that their faces were right next to each other. She smelled like fragrant soap and Downey fabric softener. All of a sudden he wasn't getting the flirty vibe anymore, but something more serious.

"What's wrong with here?" Kirkpatrick replied. "I thought I was doing all right, actually."

Meadows rolled her eyes and smiled a little. "You're doing fine, cowboy. But I think you've stepped into a bigger mess than maybe you're aware of, and this is not friendly territory. I mentioned that the mayor's brother is the owner."

"Not to be obtuse, but I guess I'm not following. What's that matter?"

Meadows gestured to a window up above the porch, which would have been on the second story inside Jackson's. "Because the only people I've ever seen use that upstairs private bar area are Jack Gables, the Burnell boys, and the mayor, and I wouldn't be surprised if one of the above is watching us from up in that window right now."

CHAPTER TWENTY-ONE

Cooper put two solids in off the break and re-chalked the cue, took a drink from his Shiner Bock. He and Davis were murdering Sancho and Bobby, and probably having a better time doing so than they should. Bobby had shown up Davis and everyone else on the wakeboard that afternoon, which left Cooper wondering if there was anything the guy wasn't good at, until he saw the guy get a few more beers in him and realized that all the stories were true, Bobby was no good with the booze.

Now it appeared they'd found something else he was bad at, though that could have been the booze's fault, too. It was like the guy flipped a switch and went from reserved super athlete to wild super buffoon.

Regardless, Cooper had forgotten how much fun Sancho could be. It had only taken an hour out on the lake before they were reminiscing on old times, telling funny stories and making everyone laugh, even Bobby, who laughed a little too hard at some moments and seemed to have something on his mind.

He had to admit he even enjoyed having to spurn Claire's advances every couple of minutes, had to catch himself from getting handsy with her once the liquor started flowing. He'd tried several times to divert her to Davis, who could use the action, but it seemed clear she was after Cooper. He almost wished Davis were enough of a cock blocker to bring up Josie and the coming baby, but he'd rather not give any more information about them than he had to, considering the circumstances. Besides, now it looked like Davis and Candace might be getting friendly anyway.

"Toss me one of them cigarettes, Coop," Sancho said. "I'll pick up a couple packs when we leave here. I don't smoke unless I'm drinking."

"Yeah? When's that?" Cooper said, smiling.

He slapped the two ball into the corner pocket, took his own cigarette from between his lips as he exhaled a cloud across the table. "I can't remember the last time I met anyone who smoked when they didn't drink."

"I do," Claire broke in, "And if you don't mind..." She stared Cooper down as she took the pack from Sancho and tapped one out for herself. She came around the table with it between her lips, adding, "I just don't buy them when I know there will be boys falling all over themselves to give me one. Got a light?"

She leaned in close to him. She smelled like some sort of fruity perfume that made his neck hair stand up.

"I think one of y'all has mine," he said, trying to stay casual. Bobby shot for the nine ball and shanked it off the pocket's corner.

Claire's fingertips touched his when she took the cigarette out of his hand without asking. "That's all right," she said. "I like it this way better anyhow." She inserted the orange ember into the hollow tip of her own cigarette, gave two big puffs, still putting one hundred percent of her eye game on Cooper.

Bobby stepped between them and handed his cue to Cooper, said, "You're up," in a slurred voice. Cooper got the impression that Claire's flirting with him was starting to piss Bobby off, wondered what their relationship was. Bobby

132

had already had three Crown and Cokes since they got to the bar and the effects were starting to show on him. Cooper didn't need this girl or Bobby's alcoholism causing problems with their deal. He took the cue and slapped Bobby on the back.

"Thanks, man," he said. "I sure appreciate you taking us out and showing us a good time like this."

Bobby grumbled something Cooper couldn't hear. Cooper lined up the shot and took a couple of practice pokes at the cue ball, then drove the eight ball home, game over. "Whada y'all say we grab something to eat? I'm fucking famished. What's good around here, Mexican?"

Everyone looked at Bobby, who seemed to be staring off into space.

"Bobby?" Sancho said, snickering. "Might be that we need to get a little booger sugar, get ol' Bobby here back on his feet." Sancho gave him a nudge. "Why don't you make us a call, Bobby?" he added.

Bobby straightened, seemed to take account of where he was in space.

"I'm game," Claire cut in.

"Let's go to Vernon's," Bobby said. "They got good brisket sandwiches, and there might be a guy there who can help us out."

Cooper and Davis exchanged looks. Davis probably felt as uncomfortable as Cooper did about letting the party go too far. Problem was, they were both having a good time. Maybe the food would cool everyone off.

"Barbecue sounds good to me," Cooper said. "And I don't suppose I'd turn down a line or two." He knew he probably shouldn't be encouraging the party, but that was the thing about cocaine: it had an allure that was almost impossible to resist, once you'd had enough to drink.

CHAPTER TWENTY-TWO

Bobby hoped Sheldon would be at Vernon's. Man, he could use a fucking line right now, just a little something to sober him up a bit. Sheldon was the only guy he could think of who would consider selling him some chach, even though Troy had forbade it. Troy didn't have the same pull with the blacks who lived north of Finney Avenue. Jack Gables had his hands in most of the business, but he didn't know all the small-time black guys, like Sheldon.

Bobby had played ball with Sheldon's much younger half-brother Russell back in high school. Guy was a hell of a tailback, only person on the team as fast as Bobby. Probably could have played division one college ball if not for his grades and criminal record.

Instead he was doing a couple of years down in the Stevenson Unit down in Cuero, while Bobby got to go be a star at UT, even though they were essentially into all the same shit. Only difference was, whenever Bobby had gotten caught slipping, his father had been there to bail him out. Bobby had never met Brandon's parents, wondered if he even had parents. Sheldon had hung around Vernon's since Bobby could remember, had even hooked him up with drugs back in the day, too. He always seemed to know where to find something.

Bobby had reconnected with Sheldon after he came home with his tail good and tucked. Sheldon still liked to hustle the pool tables at Vernon's, just like old times, when he wasn't slanging yayo in the bathroom stall. Bobby never could tell if the owner, Vernon Miles, was hip to it, but the guy always kept a low profile, stayed out of other people's business either way, so long as they weren't making waves.

Vernon and Bobby's daddy had been friends, meaning Bobby had grown up eating hunger hanger sandwiches, which was what Vernon called his brisket sandwich with pickles and onions, while his father shot pool and drank whiskey. The rest of his family never went near places run by black folks, and Bobby figured it had felt as much like an escape for his father as it did for him now.

"You good to drive?" Bobby asked Sancho as the valet pulled up with his suburban. Sancho gave him a look that said he wasn't interested in testing the DWI leniency in town a second time.

"I can drive," Cooper said. "Y'all been lapping me on the beers anyway."

Bobby nodded. "Sounds good," he said, letting the valet give Cooper the keys instead. Bobby took shotgun as Cooper adjusted the driver's seat. At least this way he could keep the guy up front with him instead of in the back end with his hand up Claire's skirt. Girl was bound to end up with something up there one way or another, and he'd still like it to be him, if possible.

"Just tell me where to go, I guess," Cooper said. "Ain't got a smartphone or I'd just map it."

"Make a right up there on Broad Street," Bobby said, his mind still feeling a little foggy from the drinks. Why did he always have to drink them so goddamned fast?

"Y'all gonna turn some music on or what?" Claire said from the third-row seat. She and Candace were in the back with their faces in compact mirrors, reapplying their make-up. Bobby hit the button and Waylon Jennings came through the speakers.

"Ew, no," Claire said.

"Definitely not," Candace added. "Here, plug my phone in." She passed her phone to the front and Bobby reluctantly took it and plugged it into the auxiliary cord sticking out of the center console. He hit play, and bass from the custom twelve-inch subwoofer in the back kicked into gear. The girls cheered. Bobby watched in the mirror as they mock twerked in their seat, Sancho pretending to make it rain bills on them the whole time. Even Davis, the quiet one Bobby had barely said three words to, started bobbing his head to the song, some trashy rap Bobby didn't remember the name of.

The song reminded him of going to the club the night Jacksonville drafted him. Last good time he could remember having. He'd fucked three different strippers in the champagne room and woke up with friction burns on his dick. Wasn't two days later, soon as he got back to Texas, that he had the accident and closed the door forever on that future. Fuck, man. That could have been his life. Instead he was jockeying for position against some no-name amateur who didn't even realize he was about to get his shit stole for the trouble. Bobby was starting to feel a lot less bad for the guy. He wondered if Sheldon would have a couple of eight balls, or if he'd have to buy it all in grams.

As soon as Bobby got through the front door he spotted Sheldon and they locked eyes. Sheldon nodded and grinned, started to go back to playing pool until he noticed Claire and Candace making a lot of noise behind Bobby, dancing around.

"Smells great," Davis said.

"I'm liable to eat myself sick in here," Cooper added.

"It's super dank. We ate here last night, played some pool," Sancho informed them.

Bobby ignored them and made his way across the room to Sheldon.

"Wussup, Bobby," Sheldon said, giving him a quick dab, then using the lighter in his hand to light a cigarette. Vernon's was one of the last places in the county besides Jackson's private room that would still let you smoke inside in spite of the smoking ban, because the smoke that seeped into the room from the resting pits behind the counter pretty well covered it. Bobby had started smoking since the accident, thought about asking Sheldon for one, but didn't. He hated the way people looked at him when he smoked in public.

"Yo, Sheldon," Bobby said. "How you livin'??"

"Shit, hustling these rednecks out of they pool money. You hosting some kind of honkey party or some shit? I see you got Claire and Candace wichu, as usual. That give me a good idea why you here."

"Everybody's a detective now," Bobby said, trying not to take it personal that Sheldon was suggesting they only hung out with him for drugs. Hell, he was probably right, anyway. Bobby couldn't think of any other reason why anyone would hang out with him anymore. "Can you help me out?"

Sheldon scanned the room to see who was watching him. The rednecks he was playing pool with moved to the other side of the table, pretended not to be interested in what Sheldon and Bobby were up to, even though Bobby could tell they recognized him. "Yeah, I got you, sure. Just don't be having yo crazy-ass uncle show up here trying to beat the shit out of me. That motherfucker's fucked up in the head."

"Don't worry, Troy don't need to know nothing about this."

"Uh huh. Just remember you said that shit. Have your people get up on some food then come see me in the bathroom, I be there in a few."

Bobby nodded. Sheldon turned back to the pool table. "Y'all be making this shit too fucking easy," he said, flashing a big smile at his opponents as he slammed the eight ball into the corner pocket. "Pay up," he added, his cigarette dangling from his lip.

Bobby made his way back to the front. "Y'all get a couple pitchers with the food," he called to Sancho, who was at the front of the line ordering. Sancho grinned at him, nodded to the young black girl working the register, who was almost certainly too young to be in the place. Bobby watched as Sheldon made his way between tables over to the bathroom. He tried to look casual as he made his way over to where Davis and Candace were already sitting. It felt like half the people in the restaurant knew what he was up to, and the other half who he was. Maybe he wasn't cut out for a life of crime. Hard to get your hands dirty when everyone is rubbernecking to get a look at you all the time.

Sancho and Cooper came and sat down with a couple of pitchers of Shiner Bock. Vernon Milescame out of the swinging door to the kitchen with two trays full of food, set them down in front of Davis and Candace.

"You folks doin' all right this evening?" he asked.

They all nodded their heads. Sancho was already filling up pint glasses and passing them around. "How 'bout you, Mr. Burnell, anything you need?" Bobby looked up eye-to-eye with Vernon. He couldn't remember when the man had stopped calling him Bobby, but apparently he was "Mr. Burnell" now.

"I'm good, Vernon, thanks," was all he said, wanting the barrel-chested motherfucker to stop looking at him like it wasa shame he still existed. Vernon had always been friendly to him back in high school, when his father was still around. Now the asshole was like everybody else, looking down his big black nose at Bobby.

"I'll appreciate if you stay that way, then," Vernon said, looking casual, eyes still locked on Bobby. Bobby was about to ask him what his fucking problem was when he remembered it. They'd gotten a little wild the other night, left this place half blacked out. He strained to remember if he'd said anything shitty to Vernon, couldn't remember, which made him realize that he'd finally reached the level where he fucked up so much and so often he couldn't keep track of it all.

"I get where you're coming from, Vernon."

Vernon nodded, turned and headed back into the kitchen, came back with two more trays of food.

"Can we get another pitcher of Shiner, too?" Sancho said to Vernon after he set down the trays.

Vernon nodded again. "You have to come get it yourself at the register, son," he said. He looked at Bobby again and made his way back over to the counter.

Bobby was about to say something shitty to Vernon when Sheldon plopped down beside him, tossed a couple of baggies into his lap.

"Two teeners enough for you?" he said in a low voice. "I decided fuck the bathroom."

Bobby nodded. "How much?"

"I'll charge it like a ball. A bill fifty."

Bobby tried not to register any outrage at the price, even though it pissed him off to be buying stepped-on coke at retail prices that his uncle probably brought uncut into the county anyway.

Sancho stood to go and grab another pitcher, but raised his glass to the table. "Cheers to friends, old and new," he said. Everyone raised their glasses so Bobby did too, even though the word friends made him want to bring the glass down upside his own head instead of drinking it. Bobby couldn't have friends now, not any more than he could have family. Those times were gone and he needed to get used to it. He clanked glasses with the group and downed his entire beer, then stood up to head to the bathroom for a key-bump.

CHAPTER TWENTY-THREE

Kirkpatrick's phone rang just as he and Meadows were headed for the front door.

"What's up, Javi?" he said into it, already knowing what was probably up.

"Our boys are on the move, so I had to leave you behind."

"All good, I'll catch a ride on my end, keep me posted on where you end up and I'll come meet you." He could almost hear Perez grinning through the phone. "Anything else?" he said.

"Try to make sure your ride doesn't last too long. We've got work to do, right?"

Kirkpatrick snickered and hung up without saying anything. Meadows shot him the side eye. "Something I should know about?" she asked as they neared the front door.

"If it's not too much trouble, I could use a ride."

It was Meadows's turn to smile now. "Be my pleasure," she said. "You can fill me in on everything on the way."

Kirkpatrick nodded and followed her, trying not to act too much like a cat in heat. She was flirting with him, sure, but he also saw the cop look in her eye when she said he could fill her in. Meadows was as much on the case as she was into him, and probably more. He wasn't sure how much to say, but his instinct said he could trust her, that she might be able to help, even.

"It's this one here," she said, gesturing to a blue Geo Prism.

"Now how am I supposed to fit into this little worm burner?" Kirkpatrick said.

"I'm not sure," Meadows replied. "But probably better than you fit into walking home."

Kirkpatrick made the sizzle noise, shook his hand like he'd touched a hot stove.

"You're kinda ornery, you know that?" he said.

"Men think any woman who knows her own business is ornery. Nothing I can do about making you better thinkers." Meadows unlocked the driver's side door and got inside, then reached across and popped Kirkpatrick's lock up. He made a show of squeezing himself in, watched her to make sure she found it amusing.

"You're kinda goofy, you know that?" she said.

"And here I thought it was one of my best qualities."

"I don't doubt it. Where we headed, *Ranger?*" Meadows started the engine, which turned over a few times before catching.

Kirkpatrick wondered what she'd say if he told her the motel, decided against it.

"You know somewhere quiet we can get some coffee?" he said instead. "I'd like to fill you in right on things, see if maybe you can help me out."

"We can go to Delroy's, it's an all-night diner and coffee house out toward the interstate, probably the only one Sheriff's Department employees won't go near. Some grievance from way back that I don't totally get the gist of. Anyway, we should be able to speak freely there."

"I'm game if you are, just let me let my man know what the deal is."

Kirkpatrick dialed Javi on the way to the coffee house,

endured another round of teasing that he was pretty sure Meadows heard through the phone, and then agreed that Javi would call him if anything changed, but it didn't look like they were out doing any deals at the moment. When they hung up, Meadows was giving him the mischievous side eye again.

"Why do you keep looking at me like that?" Kirkpatrick said.

"Like what?" "Like a lion at the watering hole."

"Like a what?"

"Never mind, you just look like I'm amusing you, is all."

"You are amusing me. And I've got a few things to say that I think might amuse you, too. Thing is, I'm not sure if I can trust you enough to tell them."

Kirkpatrick straightened up, got serious. "Girl, you've never met anyone you can trust more than me," he said.

Meadows parroted it back to him in a thick imitation of his voice.

"Ouch, what's with the claws?" Kirkpatrick said.

"It's just, the way you talk amuses me most of all. I can't decide if you're trying to pump me for information or get in my panties."

Kirkpatrick managed not to blush, thank God. "Would you kick me out of the car if I admitted it was a little bit of both? Of course, I don't have to get all the way in, you understand. I'd be willing to settle for a kiss and some cuddles."

Meadows laughed, and the look she gave him this time could not possibly have been mistaken for anything but flirting.

They pulled up to the coffee house and parked out front. There were no other cars, and you could see through the windows that there were no customers in any of the booths. They went inside and a middle-aged waitress in a

143

pink throwback uniform led them to one of the empty booths by the windows. She poured them each a glass of water and dropped a couple of menus in front of them, then moved off toward the kitchen.

"What's good here?" Kirkpatrick asked.

"Far as I know? Everything. They have a buffet in the morning that looks like my grandmother cooked it up. Back when I was on a beat I used to come grab coffee here to get away from the boys' club at the usual sheriff hangouts. One of the things that got Jack Gables sore at me, I think. Besides my having a vagina he can't touch, of course. That makes him furious."

"Maybe you should tell me a little more about the sheriff," Kirkpatrick said. "I've heard rumors that he's crooked, but I have a hard time believing a man who managed to stay in office that long could be up to too much dirt."

Obviously you're not into politics," Meadows said. "Anyway, you first."

"Me first what?"

"You tell me all about your little operation down here, and then, based on what you have to say, I'll decide what I feel like telling you. Like I said, I've got a lot I could tell, provided I feel safe to tell it."

"All right, fine," Kirkpatrick said.

"I'm on a one-man special task force. As you know, I'm after Elroy Watts. What you don't know is why."

He started to explain how Weldon Robb used his connections to pull him onto the case, and why, but she cut him off.

"I remember that," she said, excited. "I read about his grandson's suicide in *Texas Monthly*. They alluded to psychedelic drug use, but the toxicology was never released."

"He was high on some sort of psilocybin mushroom extract when he died, or so they think. Of course the senator is convinced that the substance all but put a demon in his mind, was adamant that we find out who manufactured it, which he assumed wouldn't be too hard since it was such a rare form of the drug. And that was pretty accurate, actually. We managed to trace the sale back to Elroy Watts, but could never pin anything on him. After watching him work, I'm not convinced he was the one manufacturing the stuff, but he was at least bringing it in and dealing it. Anyhow, when the heat got turned up, Watts bailed to Costa Rica, and I thought we'd heard the last of him. Then last week he popped back up on the wiretap we kept on his family ranch's phone, making a drug deal with a couple knuckleheads from up in Colorado, to bring a bunch of high-grade cannabis down here and sell it. My job is to make sure he succeeds just enough to hang himself. Now that the senator knows Bobby Burnell is involved, he's foaming at the mouth to bury them both under the jail ASAP."

Kirkpatrick sat back, let that sink in a little bit. The waitress came by and dropped off a couple of mugs of coffee, asked if they were ready to order.

"Not just yet, thanks," Meadows said, her hands folded now around the warm coffee mug.

The waitress shrugged and said, "Take your time," in a way that suggested she'd rather they not be there in the first place, went back to refilling sugar caddies.

"Why does he care about Burnell so much?" Meadows asked.

"He's a lifelong Aggie's fan. A&M made a big play for Bobby back when he was coming out of high school. I think he was some sort of all American, took Lee High School to a state championship. As I understand it, his whole family are Aggie fans, so they were royally pissed when he went to

UT, where he promptly beat the stuffing out of A&M every time they played throughout his whole career."

"Boys and their dick-measuring bullshit," Meadows said.

Kirkpatrick raised his eyebrow. "You've got a bit of a mouth, huh?" He smiled to show her he was joking. She didn't smile back. "What, something I said?" he added, feeling uncomfortable now.

Meadows sighed, seemed to relax a little. "No, it's not you. It's just men cuss and tell nasty stories about their wives around the water cooler, but if a woman uses a couple curse words, she's 'got a mouth.' It's not your fault, but I'm dealing with a lot of sexism at the job. In East Texas a woman is supposed to be seen, and only heard when she's got a man on top of her. Not the way my momma raised me, though."

"I get it," Kirkpatrick replied. "Lot of sexism in the job. Just know I didn't mean anything by it. I should watch it with that stuff, I suppose."

"Lot of sexism in the whole world, it's just more obvious in the job. I know you didn't mean anything by it. Be better if you just didn't do it, though. Anyway, so when's this deal supposed to be going down?"

"Funny thing. We were able to figure out the unsub's identity from the wiretap. Then, when me and my man Perez showed up down here, would you believe the guys were staying at the same motel, in the room right above us? Not sure when the deal is on, but we know where they stashed the pot. Long as we stay on them, we'll get em sooner or later."

"Yeah? So where do I factor in?"

"I was hoping you might be able to tell me that. I told you my song and dance, now it's your turn to unburden. Jack Gables: spill the beans. I'd like to understand how a couple guys picked up on DWI and drug possession get out of jail without talking to a judge first."

Meadows looked around the room, even though she'd already done it at least four times. Whatever she was holding on to, it made her paranoid to say it out loud. "Jack Gables is a criminal," she said. "I haven't got any hard proof of that, other than he's always cahootsing around with the Burnells, and I can guarantee you they're criminals. Bobby and your man Watts were released without charges, that's why they never saw a judge."

"I figured it was something like that," Kirkpatrick said. Meadows gave him a look that said she didn't care what he figured, and definitely didn't care for being interrupted. "Please, continue."

"Why thank you, Your Majesty, that means a lot."

"Sorry," Kirkpatrick said.

Meadows rolled her eyes and continued. "Anyway. If your guys are doing a deal with Bobby, that means they're working with his uncle Troy Burnell. Guy is one of the biggest scumbags I've ever seen. Kind of guy that wears Affliction T-shirts, slicks his hair back and gets spray tans. But more importantly, if they're working with Troy, then I'd bet the farm they're working with Jack Gables, whether they know it or not."

Kirkpatrick leaned on both his forearms now, more than interested in what Meadows had to say.

Meadows winked at him. "Good to see I've got your attention," she said. Kirkpatrick couldn't imagine anyone having more of his attention in that moment, but he resisted the urge to say it.

"So would you say this is your way of warning me of the danger?" Kirkpatrick asked.

"This is my way of telling you that crooked sheriffs probably aren't in the business of buying drugs from people they can just as easily arrest and take them from."

The idea just about slapped Kirkpatrick across the face. "Shit," he said. "I see what you mean."

Meadows smiled. "Good," she said. "Then you probably also see why you need my help if you're going to get your man."

CHAPTER TWENTY-FOUR

On your mark...get set...go!" Sancho called out.

Cooper leaned over the plate and snorted up the gagger, held the lighter to the bong's stem and sucked up a tube full of smoke, cleared it, then knocked back a shot of bourbon before he exhaled. Candace and Claire cheered as he started choking and coughing. When he cleared the tears out of his eyes enough to see, he saw Davis's grinning face, looking like a pig in shit with his arm around Candace, her hand in his lap right next to his package.

"I see you still got it, Coop," Sancho said, slapping him on the back. He turned to Bobby, added, "Coop used to be the only other guy on tour who could keep up with me. Coop, you remember that time when we took over that motel in Moses Lake, by the Gorge, had a motel-wide party?"

"Room 101 for cokestacy, 201 for extacane," Cooper said, laughing.

"We went outside as the sun was coming up, and Gina and Sneaky Pete were doing yoga in the grass by the pool." Sancho laughed too.

"That was good times," Davis said. "Even if I did pass out before most of the fun happened."

"What's the difference in cokestacy and extacane?" Claire asked.

Cooper grinned. "The room number," he said, then he,

Davis and Sancho all busted out laughing, were soon joined by the rest of them, even Bobby, who had been crabby but was loosening up now that they were gacked up. Bobby was lining up his own drug relay now, another shot, another line, and a fat bong hit.

Cooper's teeth were chattering from the blow. He'd forgotten how much better it was in Texas than back in Colorado, where it was usually pretty stepped on.

"Let's shoot some pool," Sancho said.

"I'm in," Cooper replied, feeling antsy, hoping the pool cue would give him something to do with his hands that would keep them away from Claire, who was doing her best to stay all over him. He loved Josie, was in no position to be messing around with this girl, however fine and willing she was. Plus he figured that might be what was making Bobby so grumpy. In all his life he never would have thought he'd be in the position of trying not to steal a girl from a guy who was practically his sports hero.

Cooper racked up the balls with Claire still pretty much attached to his hip. Sancho broke but didn't pocket anything. Bobby leaned against the wall as Cooper moved to line up his shot. Davis and Candace hadn't come in from the other room, and Cooper had a pretty good idea of what they were up to. He sank two solids before missing a third, passed his stick to Claire, who had insisted on being his teammate. Bobby stepped up to the table and knocked a couple of balls around, but was too fucked up to hit anything. Davis came in from the kitchen with lipstick traces on his mouth.

"Got some sauce on your face there, Davis," Sancho said, slipping on a pair of Elvis sunglasses that he must have brought with him. Davis turned even redder than the cocaine had already made him, frogged Sancho in the arm. Candace smiled like it didn't bother her in the least. Sancho unplugged Candace's phone. Her playlist had ended while they were recharging on the lines. He plugged his phone into the stereo and turned on some Panic.

"That's more like it," Cooper said, pocketing another ball.

"Anybody wanna come smoke?" Claire asked. The words were barely out of her mouth before pool cues were leaned against the walls and everyone, including Bobby, had piled out onto the back deck. Claire passed Cooper's pack around and they each took one out. Even Bobby, a world-class athlete not long ago, lit one up. Cooper figured it must have been hard on the guy, losing it all like that. He didn't blame him for picking up a few bad habits, even if he'd probably already had some of them before. Even if some of them had just about destroyed his life.

Cooper sat on the wooden benches that lined the deck. Claire tried to sit in his lap but he managed to deflect her with his hands, pushed her onto the bench beside him. Everyone else looked too high to notice. Davis was asking Bobby more questions about his college days, and Sancho seemed to be on another planet, looked like a disco dancer with his big fro and Elvis shades.

"What's with you?" Claire asked.

"Nothing to do with you," Cooper said, "I just got a girl back home."

Claire touched his hand and gave him a look that could drown a muskrat. "What's that got to do with right here, right now?" she asked.

"Actually, everything, but I don't want to get into it. You seem like a nice girl, and you're certainly something to look at, so I hope you won't take it personal."

Claire frowned. "How does a person not take something like that personal?" she asked.

Cooper shrugged, pulled on his smoke. He shifted his

focus to Davis, who had stopped badgering Bobby and shifted his own focus to Candace. His heart thumped, and he hoped he didn't look as sweaty as Davis. Cooper remembered all this stuff being a lot more fun than it all of a sudden felt. Knowing Josie was pregnant put a new filter on everything, even fun. He wanted to call her, hear her voice, but knew it was a bad idea. Still it pulled at him, then some more, and almost before he knew what he was doing he had stepped inside and was dialing her number.

She answered on the third ring.

"Cooper, you okay?"

Cooper hesitated, realized all at once what a bad idea this was. He hadn't even checked the time. "Yeah, baby, it's me," he said, trying to keep the slur out of his voice.

"Is everything okay?" Josie asked again.

"Of course, everything's fine. I—I just wanted to hear your voice."

Josie sighed into the phone. Cooper felt electricity in his fingertips so intense he almost dropped the phone. All of sudden he felt spun, was starting to wonder if Sancho had dosed him, maybe.

"You sound fucked up, Cooper."

"I'm all right," Cooper started in, but she cut him off.

"It's two-thirty in the morning here. That means it's three-thirty there. I was asleep. Did you want something?"

Cooper winced, wishing he could just hang up. Instead, he searched for the right thing to say. "Okay, maybe I'm a little fucked up," he said. "But I miss you and wanted to check in."

"Is everything done?" Josie asked.

Cooper rubbed back the tears that were suddenly welling in his eyes.

"Everything's fine. It'll be done by tomorrow evening. Then I promise I'm coming back there and getting my shit together. This ain't what it used to be."

Josie's voice sounded tired. "Just hold off on the promises until everything's done. We can talk then."

Cooper started to say something but the door to the bedroom he'd ducked off into came open.

"Hey, Cooper, where are you?" Claire said as she walked in.

Cooper could almost touch the vibe that came through the phone from Josie.

"Who is that?" she asked.

"Nobody," Cooper replied, shoving away Claire, who was trying to wrap her arms around his waist. "Just some girl Sancho's got over here."

"Sounds like somebody to me, Cooper. Are you seriously out partying with Sancho after everything we talked about? You not learn your lesson last time, or what?"

"Is that your girlfriend, Cooper?" Claire asked, butting in. "Tell her I said hi," she said in a throaty tone.

Cooper wanted to say something else but Josie had already hung up. Claire ran her hand down and squeezed his cock. He shoved her away onto the bed.

"Oh, you like it like that?" she said, curling up on her side like a snake. "I can do rough."

"Not with me you can't," Cooper said, hitting the button to redial Josie. The call went straight to voicemail.

"Thanks a bunch," he said to Claire. "You just caused me all kinds of shit. That's what you were going for, right?"

"I'm going for you, actually," Claire said. Cooper turned to leave.

"Cooper, wait," Claire called out. He turned back to face her. "She's gonna be mad either way, right? Why not have a little fun if she's gonna think you did either way?"

Cooper's face burned, and he had to take a few deep

breaths. "Problem is I'd know it was true that way, and I can't live with that." He closed the door behind him and headed back out to the porch to smoke another cigarette, figure out what he ought to do next.

CHAPTER TWENTY-FIVE

"What's shakin', Javi?" Kirkpatrick said as he climbed into the passenger seat of Meadows's car.

"Nothing shaking, that's what," Javi replied. "These suckers are in for the night, you ask me."

"I don't doubt it. Anyone new show up?"

"Nah. Same crew. They're partying, far as I can tell. You find anything on your end, besides some action?"

Kirkpatrick looked at Meadows, held back a smile, even though Javi couldn't have seen it, and he didn't think Meadows had heard the comment. "I did, actually," he said, all business. "Sounds like we could be swimming in a deeper pond than we thought. Anyway, I'll brief you on it back at the motel in the morning."

Javi sighed into the phone. "Tell me you're not gonna make me sit out here all night waiting on them to move?"

"I could tell you, but that won't make it true."

"Come on, KP, help me out, man. I'm tired. My back hurts from sitting in this goddamn car seat."

"I'm just giving you grief, Javi, jeez. Tell you what. Stay another hour, then come back to the motel and I'll switch out with you. Them boys ain't doing any deals at three o'clock in the morning, I don't imagine. I just want to make sure we don't miss the deal. No idea why it hasn't already been made."

"You want me to stay another hour because you're

sleepin' or lovin'?"

"Not sure just yet," Kirkpatrick said. "See you in an hour, compadre."

"Adios," Perez said.

Kirkpatrick clicked his phone to sleep and sat back in the seat.

"So, where to?" Meadows said. Kirkpatrick let himself grin this time.

"How 'bout your place?" he said. Meadows gave him a look that made him hold both hands out in front of him, palms forward, and add, "I'm joking. Don't shoot, Officer."

"You're full of it," Meadows said, swatting him on the shoulder. "All cops have the same two things on their minds."

"Yeah, what are they?"

"Fighting and fucking," Meadows replied. She raised an eyebrow at Kirkpatrick.

"I prefer lovin', but I won't argue semantics with you. You don't want to give me some sugar, not much I can say. I'd offer to fight you for it but I'm pretty sure I'd lose."

"Remind me, what hotel are you staying at?" Meadows asked.

"Rose City Motel."

"Y'all are staying in that dump? Why?"

"Senator Robb's tighter than Tinkerbelle, and we weren't too keen on ponying up out of pocket."

"I'd almost let you stay at my place out of pity." Kirkpatrick opened his mouth to say something, but she cut him off by adding, "Almost."

He nodded and looked out the window instead. He was having fun flirting with her, but it didn't have to go any further than that. Relationships between cops almost never worked out. Not that he was ready for one anyway, nor did he assume she was, either. He'd be satisfied if he could get a kiss and then a couple of minutes of sleep before Javi came and made him take over the watch.

Meadows turned into the parking lot of the Rose City Motel and parked. "Could probably write three or four DWI's right there," she said, gesturing at the drive-through line at the Whataburger next door, which wrapped all the way around the building."

"You do anything else besides work?" Kirkpatrick teased her.

"Not lately," she said, "But I'm thinking about making an exception." Kirkpatrick was getting ready to ask her what she had in mind when she leaned across and gave him a big, open-mouthed kiss. He kissed her back, taking in the sweet scent of soap mixed with her natural scent, which had been making him sweat for the last two hours. They made out like a couple of teenagers for a while before she pulled away.

"I've been wanting to do that since you scared off my date earlier," she said softly.

"I've been wanting you do to want to do that since the first second I walked into your station."

Meadows hit the unlock button, gave him a look no man could mistake for anything else.

"So this is goodnight?" he asked.

"I hope not. How long before your partner comes back?"

"About forty-five minutes, give or take. Why?"

"Because I don't imagine it will take us half that long to do what I've got in mind. Now which room is yours?"

Kirkpatrick didn't need to be told twice what that meant. He got out as Meadows shut off the engine, took her by the hand and led her up the stairs. Man, he hoped Perez didn't decide to come back early just to pay him back for the wrecked Camaro. By the time he got his key in the door and swung it open, he and Meadows were all over each other. He guided her over and eased her down onto his unmade bed, figuring that even if Perez came in at this point he wouldn't be able to stop himself.

CHAPTER TWENTY-SIX

Bobby woke up almost by instinct, interrupted from the same dream he had nearly twice a week, him scrambling, ducking some giant defensive end and diving with the ball into the end zone, bringing the Vince Lombardi home to Carolina like he'd brought the national championship back to Austin. The problem was that the dream always ended the same way, with him waking up back in the shit heap his life had become.

He sat up, confused at the contrast between the way he'd felt in the dream, and the sharp pain of dehydration pulsing to the rhythm of his heartbeat inside his temples. He turned over to find himself face to face with Claire's heart-shaped ass and a slimy used condom stuck to her lower back. He barely remembered the fucking, but then, he'd done it with Claire so many times it was hardly memorable either way.

He was just easing out of the bed when he realized what had awakened him. He looked down as his phone vibrated and lit up again on the floor next to the bed. His headache throbbed even faster when the caller ID confirmed his suspicion. Troy's number. "Motherfucker," Bobby said to himself, then wished he hadn't when Claire stirred and turned over, looked at him through hazy bloodshot eyes.

"Who is it?" she groaned. "What happened?"

"Go back to bed, it's nothing," Bobby replied. He slipped

out the door into the hallway, hoping she wouldn't follow him, which was silly because the chances of Claire getting out of bed before noon even when she wasn't hung over were pretty low. He slid the glass door to the back porch open and stepped out onto the deck as he dialed Troy's number.

"Where you been, shithead?" Troy said, answering on the first ring.

"Sorry, Troy, I was sleepin'."

"You must still be sleeping, throwing names out over the phone. You can stop at the Shell station on the way over and pick me up a new one now."

"Way over where?"

"Goddammit, boy, open your fucking ears. We got plans to make. I'm on my way back into town now, should be there in twenty-five minutes, give or take. You better have your flunky ass waiting at my place with a new phone and a soy sugar-free latte from Starbucks, as well as a black coffee for our legal associate when I get there." Troy hung up before Bobby could say anything else.

Bobby shrugged as if to shake off the abuse, then lost control of the feeling and spiked his burner into the deck. Plastic scattered across the fading boards. Troy would make him buy a new one now, anyway. Guy was paranoid, probably snorting too much coke or something. Probably had to be when you ripped everyone off all the time. He had a feeling it would be Jack Gables with Troy, though he hoped he was wrong.

He stopped at the Shell station just down the spur from his cove on Lake Strongbow. The place was owned by a couple of towel heads, half gas station, half head shop. The counter up front had a stack of wooden dugouts like Bobby had used to smoke schwag out of back in high scool. Glass pipes lined up beneath the glass counter, though all the ones that they sold were discounted to make up for obvious deformities, the work of amateur glass blowers. They kept prepaid cell phones on a shelf behind the counter, surrounded by cigarettes.

Bobby picked up two of them, paid cash and left. The clerks never said a word to him, and it surprised him that the Southern Baptists in town let a couple of guys like that hang around selling contraband. Probably selling cigarettes to minors, too. Gables must be getting a piece of their action or something. Gables got a piece of all the action. The man was ruthless, and Bobby had hoped above all else to avoid his getting involved in the deal. Now that he was, you could guarantee things would get squirrelly.

The Starbucks drive-through was backed up around the corner, as usual. It took Bobby twenty minutes just to get through the line, and he knew Troy was going to fuck with him about it when he got there. He didn't have enough empty cup holders to get himself a coffee, so he went without.

At least twenty minutes late, he pulled into the Baby Doll's parking lot his family had used as a headquarters most of his life. He parked next to Troy's Escalade, almost getting blinded by the sun as it reflected off the gaudy truck's chrome, twenty-two-inch rims. The Escalade had a Tapout sticker the size of Bobby's torso on the back window. In some ways Bobby figured it was nice of Troy to make sure everyone knew up front what a douche bag they were running up on, even if it was the most obnoxious thing Bobby had ever seen.

Back at UT, Troy had wanted to come visit him once or twice, but Bobby had always found a way around it. He had known exactly how that would have gone. Troy acting like a bully dip shit, trashing on the Longhorns in a town of Longhorn fans. Probably cratering one of Bobby's teammates' skulls sooner or later for taking offense to things he had said just to be offensive. Bobby hadn't needed that, but he also realized now how much it had added to Troy's impression of him as snotty, and was thus directly responsible for the shit treatment he got now.

Bobby hesitated outside the glass doors, knowing there wouldn't be much of anyone inside, but needing to compose himself before getting immersed in the smell of cigarette smoke and spilled Lone Star. Finally he pulled the door open and stepped inside, leaving his shades on.

None of the newest crop of daygirls were on stage, just the one with the dyed auburn pigtails that framed her mousey face standing behind the bar, playing with her phone. Bobby tried to remember her stage name. Matilda, he thought. Luckily she barely glanced up at him from her phone, then went back to whatever she was doing.

Bobby hesitated again at the base of the stairs that led up to a door with "Champagne Room" spelled out in bulb lights above it. Troy's office was behind a steel reinforced door down a hall to the left of it. He never handled any sort of drug deal here anyway, but that didn't make him any less paranoid. He knew Troy could see him on camera, but waited a second to knock with his elbow, the coffees burning all but his finger stub on his throwing hand, a hand in which he'd never regained full feeling.

The door swung open as he raised his elbow to knock, and Troy snatched him by the front of his shirt with both hands, pulled him forward into the room and spun him to the left like he was driving a truck, twisting him over his outstretched leg, some Jiu-Jitsu move, maybe. Bobby sailed through the air, both coffees still in hand, then landed on top of them as coffee and latte exploded everywhere, scalding the front of Bobby's shirt as he landed.

"Ouch, shit!" he screamed, his skin feeling like it had touched a hot stove. "What the fuck did I do, Troy?" Bobby was afraid to stand back up with Troy still towering over him, Jack Gables sitting in civilian clothes having a good laugh at the spectacle on the corduroy couch that probably had cum stains all over it from Troy raw-dogging- strippers on it every chance he got.

"What time did I tell you to be here?"

Bobby patted his chest and stomach, surveying the damage, which wasn't all that bad, though his chest did look red when he pulled up the front of his shirt. "I had to get your fucking coffee, Starbucks line was about round the block. Now you made me spill the shit all over the god-damn place, so you tell me how that was a productive response?"

Troy soccer kicked him between the ribs, dropping Bobby back, chest down, in the coffee puddle. He wheezed for breath, thought he felt something broken in there now, couldn't get a full lung of air.

"Ooh wee, I like how you keep court, Troy," Jack Gables said, always excited whenever there was violence around. "My boys talk to me like that and I'm liable to take them out back and pistol whip 'em to death."

Troy looked down at Bobby. "That what I ought to do with you, you little shit?" he asked. "Sometimes I feel like if I crushed your skull it'd raise your I.Q. I don't know how in hell you came out of your goddamn father's jizz. That was the part of you who could play football. The rest of this, whatever it is, you got from your fucking mother. Right about now you probably thinking about running off just like she did, right?"

Bobby shook his head, thought he'd managed to find enough air to respond, but all that came out was a steamy pile of vomit, which still looked like the cans of Spaghetti-O's he had a vague memory of eating without even heating them up around 4 a.m. If Troy had been mad before, his face said he was about to go ape-shit after Bobby stopped retching.

"You nasty little motherfucker," Troy said. He leaned down and backhanded Bobby, causing him to fall into the mixture of coffee, latte and puke. "You can clean that up when we're done. Meantime, I asked you a question. You gonna run off on us, warn your little hippy friends off before the score tonight?"

Bobby managed to sit back up, wincing from the pain in his ribs. "Nah," he said. "I wasn't planning on it."

"What was that?" Troy said. "Speak up, pussy."

"I said definitely not. Come on, Troy, you don't have to whip on me like this. Far as I know we're still right on track, I thought you were bringing me over here to make a plan."

"Shit, you think this is bad, fuck up one more time and I'll turn Jack here loose on you."

Jack Gables stood and cracked his knuckles, hooked his thumbs into his belt next to his .357 lawman pistol, his custom-made old west-style sheriff's badge gleaming from the breast of his neatly-pressed white Lou Casey button-down shirt. He met the man's eyes and even the playful wink Gables gave him didn't hide the ill intentions Bobby could see the man had for him. He sat up on his haunches, put his hands palm out in front of him.

"Look, I get it. Y'all can snap your fingers and be feeding me to the pigs. Y'all could break every goddamn bone in my body if you wanted. But believe it or not, I'm loyal to my family. I want to follow in my father's footsteps. I think this could be a better long-term deal, but it ain't my job to think, I get that. Y'all want to steal it, we gonna steal it, me right up front. Maybe we could get down to discussing how that works before you finish beating the life out of me?"

Gables laughed so hard he had to clutch his gut, bend his six-five frame in half to get out the stitches. When he finished he turned to Troy and said, "Whadaya think?"

Troy's face softened as much as it was capable of, which was pretty much only from a snarl to a scowl. "Yeah, Sheriff, I guess we can take his word. For now."

"Great," Bobby said, "I appreciate the vote of confidence. Now what do y'all need me to do?"

Troy motioned for Bobby to sit on one of the stools at the small bar on one end of the office. Bobby did as instructed. Troy sat in his chair, put his feet up on the desk.

"So here's how it's gonna go down. I decided to throw you a bone and make it clean, save you a little bullshit face with whatever people you got left. It's real simple. You have your guys bring the dope out to the barn on my farm at seven sharp. Don't be late. We do the deal as normal, exchange the money for the dope, and wish them a happy Jerry day or whatever the fuck hippies celebrate."

"I thought you said we was gonna steal it?" Bobby said, confused, maybe even a touch hopeful that Troy might have had a change of heart, before remembering the motherfucker didn't have a heart.

"We are," Troy said. "Or, rather, Des Charles is gonna do it."

"How so?" Bobby asked. Jack Gables just crossed his arms, perhaps already having spoken his part, which was telling everyone how it was gonna be.

"He's gonna wait just down the road, pull them over on the way out, cash in hand, and relieve them of said cash. The sheriff here has assured me he'll be nice and cordial about it, will let them know they can bring their proof of how they got the money down to the Teller County Courthouse and get it right back. Problem is, I don't imagine they'll want to prove where they got it, so I doubt we'll be seeing them again."

Bobby sat back and folded his own arms now, then unfolded them and wiped the coffee and puke off his arms and jeans as best he could. So that's how they were gonna do it. He knew he ought to be happy that Sancho and his friends might not ever even suspect that he'd set them up this way, though they might figure it out, but all he felt was hung over.

This could let him off the hook from burning the last bridges he had left, and yet he still felt rotten about it. He kind of liked Cooper and Davis, hated to see them get fucked over. Cooper had said something about getting a fresh start with the money, something that really resonated with Bobby, actually. He had hoped to do the same thing. Now it looked as though neither one of them were likely to get anything but a fresh foot full of cow shit.

"All right, sounds good to me," Bobby said, feigning enthusiasm. "Anything else, or can I go get cleaned up?"

Troy and Gables exchanged a look. Gables shrugged, and Troy smirked.

"One more thing," Troy said, turning to Bobby. "Go get Jack and me a fresh coffee to replace the ones you spilled."

"I spilled?" Bobby said. "You're the one who pulled some weird jiu-jitsu shit and tossed me on my face. I spent thirty minutes picking those coffees up for you. I need to go get cleaned up and shower, get my head on straight for tonight."

"You certainly do," Troy said, smirking at Gables again. "Right after you go get our coffees."

CHAPTER TWENTY-SEVEN

Cooper woke up with the feeling that his entire life was finally in shambles, that he'd finally messed it up beyond repair. He sat up to find himself on the couch in Bobby's living room in nothing but his boxer briefs. He rubbed his eyes and tried to piece the previous night back together.

He hadn't meant to get so fucked up. It felt like old times, out on tour, just partying and being free and not having to give so much of a fuck all the time, be such an adult. Except he did give a fuck now, and the thought would have sobered him up if not for the massive hangover. He started to wonder where Davis was, then remembered enough to form a good idea of it. If there was any silver lining to this thing, it was that Davis had finally gotten laid. Guy needed it.

He made his way around the house, taking soft steps and poking his head around corners like a cat burglar, not wanting to awaken anyone, but already getting that gnawing feeling like they needed to get the stash out of the storage unit before the sun got up too high. What time was it, anyway? He went back in the living room for his phone, saw that it was just after ten a.m.

Today was the day, make or break. He was anxious to get the deal done, could not for the life of him figure out in the sobering light of morning why he'd let himself party so hard. After Josie had hung up on him he'd hit the bourbon pretty hard. His last memories were of swigging from the bottle, trying to drown the effects from the cocaine so that he could sleep, and watching Sancho charge out onto the deck butt naked and throw himself in the water.

He headed down the long hallway to where he thought he remembered the guest room was. He turned the knob slowly, careful not to make any more noise than necessary. Inside, Davis was sprawled out facedown and butt naked, Candace's skinny legs practically wrapped around his torso, as if they'd just passed out without even bothering to stop fucking. He smiled in spite of the deep stress he was feeling, almost wanted to go in there and wake his best friend up with a high five. Instead he shut the door and headed for the kitchen, hoping to find some sort of Advil or something. As he searched the cabinet above the sink he noticed Bobby's Suburban coming back down the driveway. Guy had to be crazy to have been up and out so early. Last night he'd been so trashed he'd barely been able to talk for several hours.

The Suburban parked on the edge of the concrete slab and Bobby emerged from the driver's side with what looked like puke on the front of his shirt. Cooper shut the cabinet and went back into the living room, sprawled out on the couch. When Bobby came in he walked through as if he didn't see Cooper, straight to the master bedroom. Cooper heard the shower kick to life, figured Bobby had gotten sick on his way to or from his trip to the store, was probably looking for medicine the same as he was.

The thought of being in motion made Cooper dry heave, force his own vomit back down into the pit of his stomach. He was just thinking that maybe he should go wake up Davis when the back door slid open and Sancho came inside, butt-naked and rubbing his eyes, but otherwise looking pretty damn casual.

"Where you been?" Cooper said, still fighting off the nausea. "And where are your clothes?"

"Slept on the hammock out on the dock. Not sure where my clothes are." He said it casual, as if it didn't really matter anyway.

"In this heat? Damn, and I thought I felt bad."

"You probably do. Not me, though, I feel like a fucking champion. Let's get the rest of these Sallys up and go get some breakfast tacos, what do you say?"

Cooper nodded, thinking no way he could eat anything, and knowing that what he really wanted to do was go pick up the stash and hide out in his motel room until it was time to make the deal. He didn't mention it. Sancho started down the hall but was met half way by Bobby in nothing but a towel, headed the opposite direction.

"Well look at you, sugar," Sancho said.

"Don't fuck with me right now, man," Bobby said, his voice tense. "And go put some fucking clothes on."

Cooper figured he was still feeling sick, didn't blame him. Not everyone was a party machine the way Sancho was.

"Somebody woke up with a crease in their crack," Sancho said. "You'd think you were the one sleeping out by the lake without getting any action last night, not me."

Bobby turned on his heels and came back into the room, got in Sancho's face. They looked ridiculous there, one in a towel, one butt-naked.

"What the fuck did I just say, bro? Huh?" He pushed Sancho, which had Cooper standing up and getting ready to get between them until Sancho smiled and stepped back.

"Bobby, you know I love you, man," Sancho said. "No need to get upset, I'm just having some fun."

Bobby still looked like he wanted to punch Sancho. Or maybe punch himself, it was hard to tell. "I'm not in the mood," was all he said. Sancho let it drop as a shirtless Davis came into the room with Candace on his heels, wearing his Driving> Disco T-shirt and her swimsuit bottoms.

"Well, look at you two love birds," Sancho said. Davis blushed and Candace put her arms around his waist as if she could care less what Sancho had to say. Claire came down the hall now, too, rubbing her eyes in nothing but coochie cutter shorts and her bra. If Josie ever got a look at the girl, there was no way she'd believe Cooper didn't fuck her.

And that was sort of the problem, he decided now. She ought to trust him more than that, no matter how bad the situation might have seemed. He'd always been faithful, passed on dozens of chances to hook up with strange girls out on the road that nobody would have ever been the wiser of, had turned them all down. The truth was he'd loved Josie from the first moment he met her, had never wanted anyone else, however much good that didn't seem to do.

"I was just talking to these boys about getting some breakfast," Sancho said. "Wada y'all think about grabbing some breakfast tacos or something?"

Claire shook her head no, said, "I can't eat this early. But y'all go ahead. I think I'm gonna head home and take a shower. You need a ride, Candace?"

It was Candace's turn to blush now. She made eye contact with Davis and the two seemed to work something out without words. "I think I'll stay and hit breakfast with the crew," she said. "I'm pretty hungry, actually."

"Bet that ain't the only thing you plan to hit," Claire said, giving her a teasing smile. Davis turned completely red. Candace didn't even flinch.

"When it's good you go back for seconds," she said, grabbing Davis's ass. "And it was *definitely* good."

Sancho cracked up at that. "Check you two out," he said. Cooper wasn't sure if he meant Candace and Davis, or Candace and Claire. He didn't clarify.

"Sorry, girlie," Bobby broke in, looking at Candace. "No can do on the breakfast with you. We have private business to discuss, so you're gonna have to take a rain-check with Davis here."

Candace frowned, looked to Davis as if to see whether he would object. Davis looked at Cooper, in turn, not sure what to do.

"Let's all go get us some tacos together, then we drop Candace off at her place and talk things over after that. Take an hour, tops, right?" Cooper said.

Bobby folded his arms, looked a little like he would like to punch in the faces of everyone in the room. He exhaled a big lungful of air instead. "Fine," he said. "There's a Torchy's Tacos here in town now, we can go there and pick some tacos up real quick. After that we got shit to do."

Everyone nodded, and Cooper felt good about avoiding a potentially embarrassing showdown for Davis. Something was up Bobby's ass, and Cooper didn't want to do anything that could jeopardize the deal. He had a reputation for moodiness, something the pregame show hosts seemed to love to discuss back when he was at UT. Cooper wanted to get this done and call Josie, let her know he was ready to come home and be a family man for life. That is, if she'd even pick up the call.

"Okay, bye y'all," Claire said, already halfway out the door. "It was nice to meet everybody."

Cooper didn't bother with waving or saying goodbye back. Girl had tried to intentionally cause problems for him, far as he was concerned. If he never saw her again it would still be too soon.

"Everybody load up in my Suburban," Bobby said. "Let's go get this shit over with, I guess."

Cooper followed right behind Candace and Davis, who were holding hands. Davis had a thing for puppy love, would probably pine for the girl for a week after they left. It was a mean thought, but Cooper just couldn't imagine anything ever working out between the two. But then again, what the hell did he know? He couldn't even keep his own relationship in order.

CHAPTER TWENTY-EIGHT

Kirkpatrick picked up the tail as they drove out of the cove in Bobby Burnell's Suburban. He let them drive past him a couple of hundred yards before turning out and giving a casual pursuit.

Weldon Robb had been calling all morning, but Kirkpatrick was in too good a mood to talk to him and spoil it. Meadows had turned out to be a perfect fit for him as a lover, and he couldn't remember the last time he'd been so fired up by a woman. It was a wonder he'd managed to get her out the door before Perez showed back up. They damn well could have passed each other turning in and out of the parking lot.

Now he'd been sitting here in his truck for seven hours, her scent still all over him. What he wouldn't give to be curled up next to her in a bed right now, fast asleep. He'd been overdoing the job for so long that he'd forgotten how good life could be under certain conditions. There damn sure had to be more out there than vendettas and drug dealers, spoiled rich kids who lost their grip on reality and left it behind at the end of jumper cables.

Much of the compassion he'd originally felt for the senator had faded off after taking so much guff from the man over the last year. Hell hath no fury like a good ol' boy scorned.

He tailed the SUV to a place called Torchy's Tacos, a

chain that he knew from Austin but didn't realize had expanded outside of the area. He could use a couple of tacos himself right about now, but couldn't risk getting made. He was fairly certain none of these idiots had any idea what was coming, but you never knew.

He dialed Perez from the parking lot, thought it was going to voicemail until Perez picked up at the last second with a drowsy, "What's up KP?"

"Rise and shine, buttercup," Kirkpatrick said. "We got a case to make."

"Buttercup, huh? Hate to see what you call your new girlfriend. It stinks like sex in here so bad I couldn't sleep for the first couple hours."

Kirkpatrick laughed. "No idea what you're talking about," he said. "Anyway, I've got eyes on our guys, wanted to roust you in case they make a move."

"They been back to pick up their stash yet?" Perez asked.

"Nope. Right now they're breakfasting with some tacos at Torchy's. You know they have those outside of Austin?"

"Please, son. I'm Mexican. Those are whitey tacos. They'll probably put one on every corner like Taco Bell the way you white people suck down fake tacos. Especially our guy Watts."

Someone beeped in on the call, and Kirkpatrick pulled the phone back from his ear to see who it was. Weldon Robb, again. "Might be true. Anyway, this place ain't but a mile or so from the motel. If you call a cab, you could probably be here before they get done. I got Senator Robb on the other line, gotta let you go."

"All right then, I guess I'll be there soon. Tell that asshole he'd better take care of my Camaro. I love that car."

Kirkpatrick clicked over.

"Senator Robb, how are you this morning?"

"Don't give me any of that superficial charm bullshit, Kirkpatrick. I been calling you all goddamn morning, you forget how to answer your phone?"

Kirkpatrick took a deep breath, told himself this was almost over, no need to make any enemies. "I'm sorry about that, Senator," he began. "I haven't been in a spot to answer the phone much today, lots of surveillance."

"So you don't have our man in custody then, I take it?"

"Nope. But the deal hasn't gone down yet either."

"How do you know that for sure?"

"Because Perez and I know where they stored the dope, and they haven't been back since."

That seemed to placate the senator a bit. Kirkpatrick let the silence hang like a fuck you sign over the conversation for a moment before adding, "Is there anything else I can do for you, Senator?"

"Yeah, there is. You can drop that half-sarcastic attitude and bring me Elroy Watts and Bobby Burnell in handcuffs and leg shackles like they on a chain gang. If you do manage to get 'em in custody, you call me first, got it? No way I want the media getting on this before I have my chance to speak with those dipshits."

"Got it," Kirkpatrick said. "Once we wrap them up, yours is the first number I'll call."

"Good. You don't wrap them up, yours is the first ticket out to pasture."

Senator Robb hung up without saying anything else. Kirkpatrick sat back in his seat and daydreamed about telling that motherfucker where he could stick the job. He'd had enough, was ready at a minimum to take a long vacation, maybe a permanent one. He'd wanted to request some backup, given the information Meadows had provided about Jack Gables maybe being involved. Scratch

175

that, it looked like they were on their own. He'd rather be all alone than call Senator Shit Head back asking for anything resembling help at this point.

He'd learned over twenty years of law enforcement just how thin the line between cops and criminals could be. There was just so much opportunity in certain aspects of the job for a person on the take. He'd always been clean, but it wouldn't surprise him if Jack Gables was dirty. There'd been quiet rumors for years in certain circles. And he trusted Meadows's instincts.

That set him to wondering how a gorgeous girl like Meadows had gotten into law enforcement in the first place. He'd have to ask her. Maybe she'd consider making the trip down to Mahahual with him, even. Most likely she would need a new job at the end of this, either way. Maybe he could lean on Senator Robb to get her something. He was running out of favors to call in himself or else he'd find something for her for sure.

Fifteen minutes later a taxi pulled up to the edge of the parking lot and Perez got out. His black Polo shirt had wrinkles like he'd slept in it. Probably had. Perez was good people. Kirkpatrick needed to be sure he got taken care of after all this.

Perez opened the passenger door and got in.

"What, you didn't bring coffee?" Kirkpatrick asked. He was running on fumes, feeling ready to just get this thing over and move on.

"I know you're kidding, so I'm not gonna answer that. They still inside?"

"I would have had to leave without you otherwise," Kirkpatrick said.

"You sure we can't call in some of the local boys for help?" Perez said. "I'm so haggard you could call me Merle at this point."

"Was that a country music reference? Maybe you are American," Kirkpatrick said, smacking him on the knee.

"Yeah, yeah, real funny. But seriously, I think we could use the backup, just in case. Especially considering the stuff about Jack Gables you mentioned last night."

Kirkpatrick frowned, rubbed his eyes. "I hear you, bud, really I do. And I got us a recruit, actually. Supposed to call her in about half an hour and she'll be around to come help us out. Problem is, I just talked to Senator Robb and he hung up before I could even consider requesting backup, so we're on our own. Honestly, I don't think he would have gotten us anything anyway, this task force teeters on every ethical line I can think of, probably doesn't want the attention."

"I get it. It doesn't make me feel any better, but if I were you I wouldn't want to call that asshole back, either. It feels like we're out here on an island all by our lonesome though. You got me into this, I just want to be sure you're on track to get me back out. No offense, obviously, but I did already lose my baby. I'd like to keep this beautiful body." Perez gestured down at his wrinkled torso.

"The Camaro will be fine, Javi. And honestly, you're looking a little soft today anyway, so it might be too late."

"You say. The ladies love me. And no matter how good they fix my ride, I'll still remember that it had to be fixed. Spoils it in some ways."

Kirkpatrick started to say something smartass, but the Torchy's front door popped open. Watts, Daniels, Davis and Burnell stepped out into the sunshine, along with one of the girls from last night. The one, Davis, appeared to have picked himself up a girlfriend along the way. Free love and all that, Kirkpatrick guessed. He put the truck in drive and waited a few seconds until they pulled out of the parking lot, then backed out to follow.

CHAPTER TWENTY-NINE

Cooper tapped his foot impatiently while Davis and Candace said their touchy-feely goodbye, which seriously had to have taken at least fifteen minutes, the two of them making out like a couple of high schoolers.

"Y'all got a name picked out yet?" Cooper said when Davis finally got back into the truck. The joke immediately made him think about Josie and his unborn child, killing the humor. Davis just smiled and looked out the window like he was high on life.

"Get you game face on, Davis," Cooper added. "Now's when things get serious. I'm figuring we pick up the stash, drive the speed limit back to the motel, load all our shit up, and head straight over to the deal. All goes well we can be back on the road to Denver before dark."

Davis sat straight up as if he suddenly realized it was almost go time. Or at least that was how Cooper had him figured, until he spoke otherwise.

"Yeah, about that, Coop. I was thinking maybe we could hang around one more night."

Cooper put the truck back in park instead of backing out, crossed his arms in front of his chest, then sighed.

"I know what you're thinking, Davis, I do. But you know how Sancho can get. I guess you didn't notice the two bloodies and a Shiner he drank at lunch? We been lucky in that he's been fairly tame thus far, but you know how he gets the deeper the bender goes. I don't want to fuck around with all that cash. I need the money. And so do you. Plus I can't risk any more trouble, I think I might already be sunk with Josie as it is."

Davis shook his head, put his hand on the dash and faced Cooper, eyes serious. "Candace said we could stay at her place. She's got an apartment, guest room and everything. We ain't even got to hang out with Sancho."

Cooper saw the dejected, sick puppy look on Davis's face and decided to take a softer track. "Brother, listen. You're my best friend. You know that. And I know how long it's been since you had a relationship, and how bad you want somebody. I know. But—"

"No, you don't," Davis said, interrupting him.

"Come again?" Cooper said, confused.

"You don't know anything about what I'm feeling, Coop, and that's the truth. I love you like a brother, too, but you spend most of your time thinking about yourself. I'm thirty years old. I've got no real skills, never had a serious relationship. I have no idea what's about to happen to me. You've always had Josie, ever since we moved up to Colorado. She's been good to you, and y'all are good for each other. But don't try to tell me for a second you understand how I feel. I like this chick, please don't stop me from taking a shot at seeing where it goes. Our sexual chemistry is—"

Now it was Cooper's turn to interrupt. "I don't need to hear that part, I get it. How 'bout this: let's get through this deal, money in hand, and then we'll see about staying over one more night. I don't think Josie is taking my calls. I need to get back as soon as I can, so no promises. But I will think on it, best I can do."

"Good enough for now," Davis said. He went back to looking out the window as Cooper backed the truck up and turned it around, drove out of the cove. He noticed that the same truck that had been parked overnight was back sitting down at the end of the cove. Seemed like a weird place to park, fisherman maybe. He shrugged it off and turned in the direction of the storage unit, his palms already sweating at the prospect of spending any amount of time with the whole harvest in the truck's toolbox.

Ten minutes later he backed in so that the truck bed was right in front of the unit. They both got out as he fumbled on the key ring for the key to the disk lock, almost had a heart attack for a second when he thought he couldn't find it. Relief flooded his body when it was there after all. The metal door made a lot of noise when he slid it up to reveal the couch and other meager contents they'd shipped down in the CRATE. Both he and Davis stepped inside the unit and pulled the door down to knee level behind them, letting just enough light in so that they could see to cut the couch open. Cooper retrieved the box cutter they'd stashed under the couch cushion and went to work. His shirt was soaked completely through with sweat before he got half the couch's back off. He hoped the heat hadn't been too hard on the stash, figured these country boys out in East Texas would probably be satisfied with the quality either way, really.

They started loading the vacuum-sealed half-pounds into a set of Rubbermaid containers they'd put in the CRATE to use for transporting the stash on this end. They had about half of them transferred when, without warning, the metal door slid up to reveal a neatly-dressed guy in boots and Wranglers with an old, misshapen Stetson pulled low over his eyes. Standing at the other corner of Cooper's truck's bed was a shorter, muscular Hispanic guy, both leaning on the taillights.

"Howdy, boys," the one in the cowboy getup said. "Y'all must be hotter than fire in there."

Cooper looked at Davis, who was frozen in place. Then

he surveyed around to see if any of the weed was visible. He didn't think so. He was about to assume they were just a couple of yokels with no tact when he looked beyond the cowboy and recognized the truck as the one he'd seen parked at the edge of the cove where Bobby Burnell's place was located. That made his heart beat so hard that his fingertips started throbbing. He was sweating so badly that someone might as well have hosed him down.

"Can we do something for you fellas?" Cooper asked, already afraid to hear the answer.

The two men exchanged looks, nodded as if they'd come to some sort of silent agreement. "Matter of fact you can," the cowboy said, pulling a pistol out from the holster Cooper hadn't noticed attached to his side, pointing it at them. "You can stop pulling that marijuana out of that couch and put your hands where I can see them."

Only when Cooper saw the cowboy pull out the gun did he notice the silver star attached to the man's belt. The sweat pouring out of his head felt like it turned to ice as he came to terms with just how fucked they probably were. He turned to gauge Davis's reaction just in time to see his friend's eyes roll back into his head as he collapsed to the unit's concrete floor.

Cooper started to move to help him but the cowboy cleared his throat, shook his head when Cooper made eye contact.

"Not that I think you'll pull anything, Mr. Daniels, but you'd best let my associate here check on your friend while you come on out here and have a little chat with me."

When the cowboy used Cooper's name, he almost passed out himself.

"Move slow and come around the couch, son," the cowboy said. "It might not seem like it now, but this is your lucky day."

CHAPTER THIRTY

Bobby tried to take a nap in the hammock out by the lake, but goddamn Sancho was already ripping lines and pounding beers, making it hard as fuck for him to keep his head straight, which he needed to do.

Not that he did. By the third time Sanch lined up a gagger Bobby had already said "fuck it," told him to line up two instead. And Lord knew cocaine was the Lay's of drugs—you could never hit just one line. After that first one he was right there with Sancho, acting more like he was on vacation than about to execute a drug deal that involved helping his psycho uncle and the county's crooked sheriff rip off people who ought to be their friends.

Two hours slipped by like they were two minutes before he realized that Cooper and Davis hadn't come back yet. Where could they be? His heart pounded out the cocaine rumba. His nerves felt so shot from the uppers that he switched from beer to bourbon.

Somewhere inside, some part of him knew that Troy would be fucking furious if he showed up drunk for the deal. But that part might as well have drowned in Lake Strongbow once the cocaine hit his bloodstream. Drugs had a way of making him not give a fuck. It was why he took them, why anyone took them, as far as he could tell.

"Where are Cooper and Davis?" he finally asked Sancho, who seemed more interested in the Allman Brothers song they had on the radio than he was in Bobby's questions. "Hey, Sanch, you hear me?"

"Huh?" Sancho said. "Oh, yeah. I'm sure they're still getting their shit from the motel. Davis mentioned they needed to check out. And who knows where they stashed all that weed."

"They been gone a long time, man."

"Have they?" Sancho asked, his head bobbing now to the beginning of some Grateful Dead song Bobby didn't want to know the name of.

"Yeah, man, that's what I meant. I know where they went, but it's been like two hours. Trust me, Uncle Troy will lose his shit if we're late for this deal."

Sancho shrugged. "I'm sure they'll be back anytime, bro. Kick back and enjoy the sunshine. No need to be all paranoid. It's like you said when you came up to Austin, he's your uncle, so it's all in the family. They'll be back."

Bobby almost wished he could explain to Sancho how it wasn't "all in the family" at all. He'd been high when he said that, putting the sale on in hopes of securing the connection. With Troy it was all in the steroids, and that crazy motherfucker took way too many of them, which was one of the reasons he scared Bobby. Running away from three-hundred-pound giants who could run the forty as fast as Bobby hadn't scared him a bit. Football had rules. The only rule Troy Burnell played by was that he always had to win and everyone else had to lose.

Combine that approach with a six-four 'roided-out gorilla with an unhealthy amount of MMA training and you had a recipe for almost constant violence.

Fucking Troy. Bobby took a swig from the bottle of Maker's Mark they hadn't finished off last night, then chased it with most of his Shiner Bock. The nerves still throbbed in his throat. He started to imagine what everyone would say about him back at UT once Sancho told them he'd ripped them off with help from the cops. Guy wasn't Albert Einstein, but Bobby figured he'd probably put it together pretty fast.

Which meant no more weekend trips away from Troy in the seclusion of Sancho's ranch in Travis County. No more orgies and wild drug binges where it felt like he'd never had anything to lose in the first place. No more having friends or getting to retain even a trace of the person he'd been just one year ago. How had he managed to fuck himself over this bad?

"Yo, dude, you all good?" Sancho said, interrupting him from the memories. "You just got super pale and shit, you need some water or something?"

"Fuck no, I don't need any water," Bobby snapped, only realizing how much tension was in his voice afterward. Bobby didn't need this guy giving him sympathy five hours before going back home and maybe ruining his last little pocket of influence in the world.

"That ain't exactly a vote of confidence, Bobby," Sancho said. "What's got you wound up so tight?"

Bobby took a deep breath, then almost laughed when he realized that what had him wound up would wind Sancho up a whole lot tighter if he told him the truth.

"Nothing, man," Bobby lied. "Just a little hung over, I guess. I haven't partied three days in a row in a long time, it's messing with me."

Sancho shook his head. "See there, Bobby. That's where you went wrong. Me, I keep a nice buzz on twenty-four-seven, three-sixty-five. Ain't failed me yet."

Bobby didn't have the energy to mention that there was very little that would fail a guy like Sancho, who had family money and a lawyer father to get him out of whatever trouble he managed to fall into. He checked the time on his phone again—2:30 p.m. They only had a couple of hours before they were supposed to meet Troy, plenty of time for Cooper and Davis to get back. He was probably just being paranoid. He took a big swig of the bourbon. "Should we line another one up?" he said.

Sancho sat up, lifted his sunglasses and smiled. "Hell, Bobby, that's the spirit," he said, already on his feet and headed toward the plate stashed in the boathouse storeroom. "We got us a motherfucking party going now."

CHAPTER THIRTY-ONE

"You boys have yourselves a good trip down from Colorado?" Kirkpatrick asked. The look on Cooper Daniel's face said that he was certainly starting to have a bad trip now. Kirkpatrick almost felt bad for them, couple of amateur hippies in over their heads, not even aware they were already drowning, though it was probably starting to dawn on them.

The boys exchanged a look, then Cooper finally said, "Y'all been following us this whole time, haven't you? Was it Nelson, did he roll on us?"

Perez moved farther into the storage unit to flank them from the side. He helped Trevor Davis sit up against the metal wall.

Kirkpatrick nodded his approval to Perez, said, "I don't know any Nelson, boys. And frankly, unless he's in the Great State of Texas committing felonies with you two dumbos and your pal Elroy Watts, I don't want to know him."

The looks on their faces said they were getting a clearer picture now.

"Should I just stand here?" Cooper Daniels asked, clearly scared. "What do y'all want us to do?"

"Well, right now I want you to walk slow past Dectective Perez over there and come on out of the unit. Normally I'd put you face down, but I can see you're having a tough day, and a hundred-fifty-degree asphalt probably won't make it any better. That said, you try anything stupid and Dectective Perez is gonna show you why he was a three-time Golden Gloves champ back in San Antonio."

Perez's face registered a tiny bit of surprise that Kirkpatrick knew that about him, then slipped right back into stone-cold cop face again. Perez waved the barrel of his Ruger SR40c toward the front of the unit. "Nice and easy, fellas," he said. "No reason to hurry or do anything sudden."

Perez probably knew these two weren't likely to put up a fight, but like Kirkpatrick, he had been wrong before. There was no telling what a man might do when staring down the barrel of a hefty stretch on a state jail felony. He almost wouldn't blame them. These two didn't exactly look cut out for a dime stretch in Huntsville.

When they made it out of the shadows of the storage unit and into daylight, Kirkpatrick had them put their hands on the wall and spread their feet. He checked them one at a time while Perez covered them, but neither had anything of merit on their person.

"Well, boys," he said. "I've got good news, and I've got bad news. Honestly, it doesn't really matter to me which one you want to hear first, but I think the good news will cheer you up just a touch, so I'll give you the bad first. The bad news is, the jig is up. We've got you on tape setting this deal up, Mr. Daniels, and though I obviously haven't tallied up all the dope you've got stashed in there, it looks like more than enough to send you both down for ten years, at least.

"Sucks, I know. But here's the good news: You two ain't the target of this thing, so I'm gonna make you the offer of a lifetime. Before I tell you what it is, I need to know whether or not you boys are committed to staying out of prison, whatever it takes. Go ahead and turn around now nice and slow, but don't do anything stupid."

Davis and Daniel's turned around, both soaked completely through their shirts with sweat.

"Can I count on you two to cooperate?"

The boys looked at each other for a long time. Daniels had tears in his eyes.

"What are y'all, FBI?" he finally asked.

"Texas Rangers," Kirkpatrick said, shifting his hip out so that they could get a better look at his badge.

"Texas Rangers...I don't get it?"

"You never heard of the Texas Rangers?" Perez broke in, almost making Kirkpatrick crack a grin through the serious face he was projecting. Sounded better than Travis County Sheriff's, this being Teller County and all.

"No—I mean yeah, I've heard of the Texas Rangers." Kirkpatrick picked up just a touch of shaking in the boy's voice as Daniels added, "My great-great grandfather was one back in the day."

"No shit?" Kirkpatrick said, his curiosity suddenly piqued. "What was his name?"

"Samuel Johnson."

"Huh. You know they've got his rifle and some of his stuff at the Texas Ranger museum in Waco, right?"

"No, I did not know that," Cooper mumbled, his tone sounding like he was on another continent in his head.

"I'll tell you what. You boys cooperate and maybe you'll get to see it for yourself without having to wait a decade down in Huntsville. I'm after your buddy Watts, you help me get him and I'll do my best to keep your time to a minimum. No promises, you understand."

Davis gasped when Kirkpatrick said the word "time," and he figured he'd almost scared them enough to get them to cooperate.

"Either of you got a lady back home or else a family?"

Davis just shook his head no, apparently too dumb-founded by the shit he'd stepped into to respond. When he looked back to Cooper Daniels, their eyes met and locked into place.

"I've got a baby on the way," Daniels said, strain in his voice. "My girl just told me she's pregnant a few days ago. Ain't that some shit? This was gonna be our last time doing anything like this. I know y'all don't believe it, but it's true. But I can't roll over on Sanch just because you caught us slipping."

"Think about your lady and your baby before you decide, son," Kirkpatrick began, Perez still covering everyone with the .40 cal, sunlight reflecting off his mirrored sunglasses, the look on his face betraying nothing. "Besides, it was your man *Sancho's* phone that led us to you to begin with, so he's got you wrapped up in it, not the other way around. I doubt he'll be volunteering to take your place, put it like that."

Daniels shook his head. "Still, it's not right. I sell my friend to the wolves, still gotta watch my other friend go to jail? Y'all might not believe it, but Davis here was just along for the ride. It's my fault he's involved. If we're gonna make a deal, let's make one. No charges for Davis, I take responsibility for the dope and help you grab your man."

Davis started to protest, but Cooper Daniels shushed him. "This is my problem, let me handle it," he said.

"But Coop—"

"Davis, you gotta trust me, buddy, now shut your mouth."

Kirkpatrick studied Daniels's face, which looked as sincere as it did serious. He got a sense that this was the right bargaining chip to get them to Watts, maybe even to some crooked cops, along with Bobby Burnout. "All right, done," Kirkpatrick said.

"I want it in writing."

"No can do, son. We need to move fast on this thing, authorization for that kind of deal will take too long. Best I can do is go to bat for you afterwards."

Daniels shook his head. "You said you wanted Sancho, am I right?"

"Yes."

"I haven't got a clue why all this fuss is about him, but I get the impression you need him. You want my help to get him, we make this deal, and no other, and we put it in writing right now. Otherwise I've got nothing else to say. Take us to jail."

Kirkpatrick thought it over, rubbed his chin. The goddamn kid had taken all of two minutes to find his power in the situation, and he was using it. Kirkpatrick respected that, kind of liked the kid, everything else aside. "I'll make a call, see what I can do," he said.

Cooper started to respond, but was cut off by the phone ringing in his pocket.

"Easy," Perez said. "Don't even think about reaching in there for it."

Cooper held his palms up higher. "I get it. But listen, this could be Sanch letting us know where the deal is going down. Maybe I ought to check?"

Kirkpatrick thought it over. "Okay, answer it," he said. "But play it cool, son, this is an important moment in your life. One wrong move and it will be the last one."

Cooper eased the phone out of his pocket and answered it with a meek, "Hello?"

The voice on the other end said something Kirkpatrick couldn't make out. He thought it sounded female, a thought Daniels confirmed when he said, "Listen, baby. Some things have happened, and I can't talk right now. I'm sorry I didn't listen to you. I'll call you when I can. I love you."

"Hang it up *now*," Kirkpatrick said, but he'd already hung up anyway. "Have you lost your mind, son? Last thing I need is your girlfriend tipping off your buddies we're coming."

"I just wanted to let her know I was in a bind. She hates Sancho, wouldn't call him if he were the last person on earth. Besides, she doesn't know what's going on anyhow. Go make your call. You give me the deal I want, I'll make sure you get what you want. I'm not here to mess anything up at this point."

Kirkpatrick couldn't argue with that, so he stepped back toward his truck and dialed Weldon Robb's number.

CHAPTER THIRTY-TWO

Bobby was finally so high he'd just about stopped worrying about the deal when Cooper and Davis pulled down the driveway in Cooper's Toyota Tundra, parked it in the shade under the big pine tree off to the side of the driveway. Bobby followed Sancho back down the pier to the driveway, slack-jawed and grinding his teeth. It looked like they'd both changed clothes. Maybe they'd decided to shower at the motel or something.

"Y'all get lost?" Sancho called out. "Guys never could find your way around on tour. I guess nothing much has changed."

"Just took longer than we thought, is all," Cooper said. He looked pale, sweaty. Bobby didn't really care how Cooper felt at this point. Soon enough this guy and all these people would be out of his life for good, like everything else. With his heart thumping in rhythm to the blow, it was hard to care about any of it, almost felt like he was doing them a favor.

"Y'all look like shit, Coop," Sancho said. "I had my suspicions you'd gone JV, now I know it's true." Neither Cooper nor Davis responded to that. Sancho added, "Come on inside and I'll tighten y'all back up with a couple gator tails. They been treating me and Bobby pretty damn good."

"No, thanks," Cooper said. "Think I'd like to just get through this deal with my head on straight."

Something had changed in the guys in the time they'd been gone, Bobby could see that even all jacked up on coke. Probably nervous about all that money and with damn good reason, really. Some part of him still felt a little sorry for them, a couple of suckers, worried their deal might go south when it might as well be sitting at the South Pole already, anyway. What kind of a drug dealer just drove somewhere with that much dope to exchange thirty Gs with a bunch of strangers, no guns or protection?

Maybe he *was* doing them a favor, giving them a reason to leave the drug game to the real criminals. The only criminal activity Bobby ever saw firsthand were things Uncle Troy and Uncle Zach did, and they were both the kind of guys who were as likely to pistol-whip you as know your name.

The thought of Troy pistol-whipping people started to get him riled up again about what had happened that morning. Motherfucker always humiliating him, always being a dick just because he could.

Bobby followed the rest of the group inside and moved past them to his bedroom, shutting the door behind him. He opened his nightstand drawer, pulled out the Baby Glock pistol that had once belonged to his mother. Why she'd left it behind he'd never known, but he was glad he still had it. He popped the full clip into it and made sure the safety was on, then set it on the bed while he put on some jeans and a pair of Asics running shoes.

He tucked the pistol in the back of his waistband. Not that he thought there would be any trouble with these guys, but as volatile as Troy could be you never knew what might happen. He just felt like it might not be a bad idea to be armed if some shit did go down. Plus he was sick and tired of Troy whipping on him all the time.

Back out in the living room, Sancho was bent over the

plate of cocaine on the coffee table, still trying to entice Cooper and Davis, who both looked like they might get sick. The one thing Bobby always had more room for, no matter how sick, was cocaine.

"All right, I get it," Sancho was saying. "Y'all are a couple of nuns on the job, no way to make it fun. What about you, Bobby, you want another gator tail?"

Bobby sniffed in a big breath, could taste the metallic chemical drip from the blow he'd already done, which made another line seem all the more enticing. Without thinking, he took the straw from Sancho and bent over the table to suck up one of the lines.

"Whoa, since when are you strapped up, Bobby?" Sancho asked. Bobby's shirt had fallen forward and revealed the pistol. He tried to be cool even though he could feel his heart pounding in his ears.

"I always carry it, or at least most of the time now," he lied, his mind scrambling for an explanation. If he scared them off now, Troy would probably beat him half to death, if not all the way. "I, you know, since the accident, people sometimes try to fuck with me. Some of them come on strong so I figured I should start carrying a pistol around."

"I don't like guns," Davis said, fear clearly written across his face. "Never have." He watched Davis and Cooper exchange a panicked look, needed to do something to help them chill out, which was hard, considering he'd done so much blow now that his teeth were damn near chattering.

Cooper said, "Sanch, what's up? Something I should be aware of? I'm with Davis, I don't care for handguns."

Bobby made eye contact with Sancho, was surprised to see his friend not even the slightest bit fazed. "I know why y'all were gone so long," Sancho said to Cooper. "Y'all must have been at church. That's why you're acting like a bunch of Sallies. The fuck do you care if Bobby's strapped? You worried we're gonna rob you?" Sancho cracked up, as if the idea of robbing them was akin to his growing wings out of his ass and flying to California. It gave Bobby an adrenaline shot, made him start to sweat a bit, faded out his buzz. Robbing them was exactly what they were going to do, Sancho just didn't know it. That was probably the only reason they were going to get through it. Sancho went over and clapped Cooper on the back. "Come on, Coop, you know I'm just fucking around. You ain't got nothing to worry about. It's Bobby's uncle we're dealing with, so it's all in the family. Right, Bobby?"

Bobby nodded his head, realizing again what a terrible fucking criminal he was turning out to be. "Exactly, all in the family," he said, taking another big sniff to get more of the cocaine to drip down his throat.

CHAPTER THIRTY-THREE

Kirkpatrick called Meadows as soon as he finished printing out the paperwork Weldon Robb faxed over to the local FedEx Office. He asked her to bring some wire transmitters so they could wire up Davis and Daniels, arranged to meet back at the motel. The agreement might not ultimately hold up in any sort of court, but these kids didn't know that, and Kirkpatrick would do his best to make things go as promised afterward. So long as Weldon Robb got Watts and Burnell, the rest ought to be easy enough to put into play, surely the man could get a prosecuting attorney to sign on to it.

Kirkpatrick had wanted to secure some additional back-up, but everyone he felt could be trusted was too far out of range to arrive in time for the deal. He figured it would be too risky for Meadows to reach out to anyone else locally. After some discussion he and Perez decided on what they thought was a good strategy, based on the information they'd gleaned off Davis and Daniels. They would wire Davis up, since he was getting the best end of the deal, then park out on the highway and make their way up to the deal site. When he told Meadows she would have to stay behind she almost took her ball and went home. Ultimately, Kirk-patrick convinced her that she would be in a better position back at the truck to see if any of Jack Gables's cronies rolled up on the deal.

Once they had it on tape, they'd ease in, make everybody assume the position, and then Meadows would come in to assist. That would be that and with any luck, Kirkpatrick could be down in Mahahual this time next week.

"So this guarantees Davis doesn't do any prison time?" Cooper asked when Kirkpatrick put the paperwork in front of him.

"Not completely, but it's the best I can do," Kirkpatrick replied. "You boys might have to testify, and that could get dangerous, I won't lie. But you play ball and do this thing and I can pretty well guarantee we will keep you both out of Huntsville. Probably a long stint of probation for you, though, Mr. Daniels."

The boys eyed each other. Davis looked scared, plain and simple. Cooper Daniels looked more resigned, determined. They seemed to have come to some sort of silent agreement and Cooper scratched his name on the appropriate line, as did Davis.

"Good choice, gentlemen," Perez said. Kirkpatrick could tell he was getting amped for the finale. Cases like these had a way of making you anxious as hell to close them out. Perez probably didn't get all that much excitement in his day-to-day position. Lowlifes, small-time drug dealers, but nothing like bagging a celebrity, making friends in high places with Weldon Robb, and maybe even taking down a crooked Sheriff in the process.

Kirkpatrick remembered when he'd felt that kind of excitement for cases. When he'd first joined the Rangers he'd been gunning to show everyone what he could do. Tracked down a serial killer who traveled the rails around Texas, knocking off prostitutes with the blunt end of a hammer, put a case so heavy on the guy he got fast-tracked to death row, was executed inside of two years.

Then he'd tracked down the daughter of an oil baron

who had been forced into being a sex slave for the Texas Syndicate. Turned out they'd taken her after her father decided to stop allowing them to traffic drugs and women across his ten-thousand-acre ranch that ran along the border outside Nuevo Laredo. Kirkpatrick was destined for stardom until his wife up and left him.

At the time it had totally blindsided him. It wasn't until later that he came to understand that an ignored woman will find someone to pay her attention no matter what you think her character is.

Not that the lesson made him feel any better. If he'd found it at the bottom of a thousand bottles of beer, it had been the only way he knew how. His work had slipped, and though he eventually got his game back on point, it was too late, he'd given the wrong impression to the people responsible for his career.

That's the reason he figured they'd pawned him off on the senator. He'd become capable again, but the slipup was just too much for the high-profile position of Texas Ranger. If they were going to have to sacrifice a man to political corruption and personal vendetta, Kirkpatrick was the perfect patsy, and even he knew it.

When Meadows arrived he stepped out to meet her at the car. He wanted to chat with her alone before letting her get around their boys, who seemed pretty jumpy.

"You brought the equipment, I take it?" Kirkpatrick said.

"You take it correct. Had a hell of a time getting it though, snuck a key from one of the narcotics officer's desk, almost got caught rooting around. Had to walk past the storeroom fifteen times before I could sneak in unseen. That's why I'm late."

"Hell, you're right on time, really."

Meadows smiled, but Kirkpatrick noticed she was definitely in business mode. "You tell them what they were walking into, or are they on a need-to-know basis, too?"

"I don't figure it will help them act natural to tell them they might be getting rolled up with a crooked sheriff, do you?"

"I doubt it. Still, you don't know Gables. They could get killed. Guy seems like he'd cut a dog's throat to watch it bleed."

Kirkpatrick shrugged, trying to pretend like he wasn't worried as much as he really was. "Chance we'll have to take," was all he said.

"Yeah, but we're not the ones taking it," Meadows replied. "But it's your show, I'm just a stagehand, anyway, from what you said on the phone."

"Please don't take that as disrespect. I know you can handle yourself. Hell, after the way you handled me last night, I'm sure you can handle anything. Truth is, I don't want to put your career at risk in case we don't hem up Jack Gables. Man who's been in his position for so long probably knows better than to be sitting there holding the bag at the moment of truth."

"I get it. But the key words there are 'my career,' meaning it's mine to mess up how I see fit." Meadows's face said she still felt like an outsider to the boys' club, but it seemed like she was accepting what needed to happen.

Kirkpatrick could feel her putting the wall up on him now, though. He shook his head. "You're right, except in this case it would be me and Javi dragging you into a situation we might not be able to cover your back about later. You know how it is, circle the wagons and all that. You could be a pariah far outside of this department."

They went inside, where Daniels and Davis were sucking on the cold Coca-Colas Javi had been decent enough to go get them from the Coke machine. Meadows took one glance at them and gave him a look that said *You're sending these guys in against Troy Burnell?*

They went over the plan together, using the timeframe and details Daniels and Davis could provide. Kirkpatrick had to admit they knew damn little, was surprised they hadn't already been robbed, bound and gagged, doing business that way. Maybe in Colorado or out on Grateful Dead tour that kind of business flew, but in his experience most deals didn't take long to get to the gunplay, especially when the person holding the dope seemed so clearly unprepared.

They decided to wire up Trevor Davis, rather than Cooper Daniels. He was the obvious leader between the two of them, so he figured it would be better to keep him clean, since he'd be doing the talking. A guy like Burnell probably didn't think these guys were anything but born victims, and Watts was their friend, meaning he trusted them. With any luck they ought to be able to make the whole thing go down relatively painlessly.

As they pushed their guys out the door and headed down the concrete stairs behind them, Kirkpatrick and Perez exchanged an unmistakable look. It was show time.

CHAPTER THIRTY-FOUR

Cooper pulled the truck up behind Bobby's Suburban outside a big, red-painted barn. They'd driven down half a mile of caliche rock road behind an iron gate with a Tapout logo emblazoned on it to get this far. Cooper didn't know who Troy Burnell was, but he didn't like the looks of anyone who kept something so tacky on the gate of what had to be a million-dollar ranch. And he really didn't like knowing that the cops who were supposed to protect him and Davis were now locked out a half-mile away.

He shut off the truck's engine and looked Davis in the eyes. The look he got back told him Davis was scared as hell, but trying to hold it together.

"We gotta lock it up," Cooper said. "I know, I'm fucking scared as hell, too. I'm sorry I got us into this, just know I'm doing my best to get us out, if I can."

"I'm all right. I just feel like this contraption they put on me is burning a hole in my clothes. Like everyone can see it or something."

"You can't even tell it's there, trust me," Cooper said, wondering if Davis would ever really trust him again after this.

"I do trust you, Coop. I know you're doing your best to handle this situation, and I appreciate you stepping in front of the bullet for me. But that don't make me feel any better about doing it, and this place fucking creeps me out."

Before Cooper could say anything else Sancho was tapping on the driver's side window. Cooper opened the door a crack.

"Y'all planning on having a heartfelt all night or you want to take care of business?" Sancho asked. "Let's get this done so we can get the party rolling again."

Cooper and Davis got out of the truck as if they were synchronized swimmers. The humid air almost felt like water as Cooper made his way to the toolbox and opened it.

"Help us carry these inside, will you?" Cooper said to Sancho. Over Sancho's shoulder he could see Bobby conversing with an angry-looking guy with gelled-up hair. That had to be Troy, if the Tapout shirt that matched the front gate was any indication. Troy had slicked-back black hair and needed a shave, the hairs on his face looking as much like a Brillo pad as whiskers.

Cooper lifted one of the Rubbermaids out of the toolbox and headed for the entrance to the barn, which was directly behind Troy Burnell.

"Cooper, Davis, this here's my uncle Troy," Bobby said in a flat, almost bored tone. It wasn't hard to see that he didn't have a better opinion of his own uncle than Cooper was getting. It would be hard to have any other impression, really. You could tell the guy was mean just by glancing at him. Cooper's heart was beating so loud that he worried people could see it moving his pearl snap up and down, pulsing a guilty rhythm. He could only imagine how Davis was feeling, being the one all wired up. He hadn't liked that idea, but the cowboy cop, Kirkpatrick, had convinced him that it made sense.

Sancho certainly knew who was in charge between himself and Davis, and Bobby had all but treated Davis like a flunky so far. Maybe he was just jealous about Candace or maybe he just didn't like Davis. Cooper had the impression he wasn't big on either of them, but business was business. If anyone was getting checked it would probably be Cooper, though. If they both got checked, well, they were probably fucked. But what reason would anyone have to check them, anyway?

Troy Burnell didn't even bother saying hello, just nodded and turned to lead them into the barn. He had the meanest eyes Cooper had seen in a long time, and that flared up his fear even more.

"Nice guy," Sancho mumbled under his breath. Troy turned back and shot him a look that a dog could have picked up on: Open your mouth again and lose your teeth. Bobby elbowed Sancho in the ribs.

"What, bro? I'm just fucking around," Sancho whispered.

"What you're doing is asking for a good ass-stomping," Bobby replied. "Troy don't fuck around, keep it in mind."

As usual, Sancho never knew when to get serious. Back in Dumas it had been the same thing, the three of them sitting on a trunk load of dope in a town where they stuck out like the Three Musketeers of Weed, and Sancho still shooting his mouth off even to the cops when they arrived. Cooper wished again he'd just listened to Josie. Or Davis. Or anyone in his life. Now Davis was caught up in his mess and they were both stuck risking their lives, not to mention narcing out a friend, which would forever crush their reputetion out on tour and everywhere else.

Worst of all, he wondered if he'd even be free when it came time for his child to be born or if Josie would be stuck explaining to people over and over again that her child's father had gotten his dumb ass locked up.

Cooper was surprised to see that the inside of the barn was completely finished, had nothing even resembling hay or animals. Instead, the barn looked like half boxing gym and half man cave, had a full MMA cage on one side with several different shapes of punching bags hung around the perimeter, and a couple of leather couches in front of a ninety-inch television on the other end. There was a full bar adjacent to the television area with bottles of every kind of liquor imaginable lined up in front of a mirror behind it, and a table next to the bar with four chairs around it.

Behind the couches was a full-sized pool table with custom felt that looked like the Texas state flag. The whole place was something a man-child would have conceptualized as a playroom.

"You boys have a seat over there," Troy said, gesturing to the couches just as a big, scary black cowboy with his jeans tucked into his boots and a prison stare that was obvious, even at a distance, came in the door, leaned in and whispered something in Troy's ear. Troy nodded and the man went back outside the way he'd come in. Cooper looked at Bobby and realized he was staring at the guy, too, looking afraid himself. Cooper's and Bobby's eyes met for a couple of seconds before Bobby looked away and Cooper's feeling suddenly went from bad to far worse. Something didn't smell right. Bobby's face said something was very wrong.

"I get you boys something to drink?" Troy Burnell said from behind Cooper, startling him back into the moment.

"I think I'm good, actually," Cooper said. "Had a couple of days' worth last night." Davis shook his head no but looked too nervous to actually say anything as Troy made his way around the couch and in front of them.

"Shit, I'll take a Crown and Coke for sure," Sancho said.

"What did you say your name was again, boy?" Troy said to Sancho.

"His name is Elroy but people call him Sancho," Bobby broke in. His nerves were unmistakable now, and Cooper's feeling that something might be wrong was growing into near certainty.

"Come on now, boys," Troy said, turning back to Cooper and Davis. "Surely y'all ain't gonna refuse my hospitality. Where's your manners? My man George out there's still got to weigh your product before we pay you out, and it might take a minute. I sent him to grab the scale. Let me get y'all a beer, at least."

Cooper shrugged and nodded, figuring it was best not to poke the bear, and wondering if that's what he'd actually sent the big cowboy guy George to do.

"Good," Troy said. "Bobby, mix up Sancho there a drink and grab a couple Lone Stars for these boys. One for me, too."

Bobby didn't move to get up and Cooper wondered if he'd even heard what his uncle had said. Troy smelled like cheap cologne and it was starting to give Cooper a headache. That or maybe the nerves. He realized for the first time that he and Davis were far from being real criminals. Sure, they'd grown a mountain of dope over the years, and made quite a lot of illegal money doing it, but that didn't mean shit.

Right about now he was realizing what real criminals looked like, and it scared the shit out of him. He'd never wanted anything so bad in his entire life as he wanted to get out of this situation, to just run for the door. And not just the situation, either. The whole game. He'd been a fool to even try and make this deal. They were caught between a rock and a hard place, and Troy Burnell looked like the kind of rock that crushed hippies from Colorado just for the fun of it.

He should have known that Sancho wasn't careful about

who he did business with or how he did business in general, for that matter. It was exactly what the Ranger, Kirkpatrick, had said. Sancho had gotten them caught in this out of pure carelessness.

Except maybe it wasn't all Sancho's fault. Cooper had been so eager to find a solution to his problem that he'd cut corners and talked on an unsecured line. All he'd wanted was to ease the anxiety he'd been feeling about Nelson getting popped, and he'd known it was a bad idea to talk on a landline, but he'd done it anyway.

Sounded like they had the whole conversation on tape now, so nothing to be done but go forward if he wanted to get out. No wonder Sancho had been down in Costa Rica for six months: he'd had some very serious cops shaking the trees all around him, not that he'd mentioned any of it to Cooper. Troy set down a sweaty Lone Star in front of him.

"Now, let's get down to business, boys," he said.

CHAPTER THIRTY-FIVE

Bobby felt the Glock's cold plastic against his back again, his sweat dripping down his pants where the slide made contact with his bare skin. Every time Troy said something shitty to him it made him want to whip it out and start shooting. Not that he had the guts for that.

He mixed up a drink for Sancho and pulled a couple of beers out of the fridge for Cooper and Davis. It wasn't so much that he was embarrassed that Troy bossed him around and wouldn't let him have a drink of his own, but more that the cocaine was starting to wear off and he needed something to balance himself out. Nothing balanced a fading coke high like whisky.

"You mixing those drinks, Bobby, or what?" Sancho called out from the couch, shaking Bobby back out of his head. "Y'all want to play some pool or something while we wait?"

Bobby looked at Troy, who was an absolute Nazi about that ridiculous Texas flag pool table. Bobby himself had never even shot so much as a single game on it. The only person he'd ever seen Troy let play on it was Jack Gables, and even then only because Jack didn't ask, just racked up the translucent balls and started shooting. No way Troy was letting a couple of guys he was about to rip off play pool on his table.

"Just sit tight right where you are," Troy said. "My man

207

will be right back. Watch the television if you get bored."

Sancho cocked his head to the side and Bobby could tell he was about to say something smartass, so he rushed around the bar and shoved the whisky drink into Sancho's hand. "Here you go, man, cheers," he said as he handed it over. Sancho took a big swig of the drink instead of saying anything, which was good because Troy was already looking at Sancho like he might bury him down by the creek that ran across the back of the property.

Bobby set the beers in front of Cooper and Davis, careful to lay out coasters so that Troy didn't freak the fuck out about the coffee table. Sancho walked over and leaned against the bar instead of heading for the pool table. Thank God. Bobby was sweating profusely now in spite of the industrial air conditioner that was currently hammering cold air into Troy's weird fucking psychopath clubhouse. Neither Cooper nor Davis moved to take a drink from their beers. They were nervous, didn't take much observation to see that. In fact, they'd been acting this way since they left to pick up their stash. Maybe their Spidey sense was tingling or maybe they were just such amateurs that they couldn't handle the heat.

Either way they were going home unpaid today, whether they realized it now or not. It still pissed Bobby off that they couldn't just do this deal the right way, but watching the two guys now, in the heat of the moment, he did have to admit that a guy like Troy couldn't in his right mind ever pay two guys like that when taking their stash was such an obvious option.

"Y'all think we can watch something besides this UFC bullshit?" Sancho asked no one in particular. Bobby winced, knowing that Troy hated it more than anything when people called MMA "UFC." Any second now he figured Troy was gonna haul off and Superman-punch Sancho across the room. Guy had always had a mouth, seemed to have absolutely no instinct for when it was time to shut the fuck up. Right now he was making Bobby so nervous that he was starting to feel less sorry about ripping his friends off.

"You just sit tight and stop asking so many goddamn questions," Troy said, his eyes boring through Sancho in a way that Bobby figured even Sancho's drunk ass could discern as imminent danger. Wrong again.

"It's just I hate this violent bullshit, bunch of ego guys taking their shirts off and trying to beat the hell out of each other for money."

"Yeah? How you feel about someone doing it for free, shutting your big fucking mouth up?" Troy asked, taking a step toward Sancho, who still seemed oblivious. Luckily, just then George came in with the scale and set it on the table adjacent to the bar, distracted Troy just enough to avoid having him start arm-barring motherfuckers.

Bobby was surprised Troy had even bothered going through the motions, figured it was Gables who wanted the thing to be clean, buy the dope, pick the money back up out on the highway, no one ever able to prove the setup and go running to the FBI, getting themselves killed in the process. If it were up to Troy, he'd probably just kill them and take the stash, bury them out back and never give it another thought.

The smell overpowered the barn as soon as George cut open the first vacuum-sealed bag, a mixture of skunk spray and diesel fuel, with fruity overtones. It was some of the strongest-smelling weed Bobby had ever smelled, meaning it was light years ahead of the Mexican schwag Troy was used to dealing by the truckload up to Dallas. The market had fallen out of that business as legalization and medical marijuana took over the whole country, pressing the supply of good, homegrown weed to unfathomable heights. It was what had given Bobby the idea to hook Troy up with Sancho to begin with. Apparently he'd forgotten that Troy had a prison mentality about this kind of thing: steal and sell the wheels off the car your friend would drive to get you both to work tomorrow if the price is right today.

"Goddamn, where y'all get this shit?" Troy asked, obviously impressed, though still not friendly.

Cooper looked like he wanted to say something, but Sancho beat him to the punch.

"Ol' Cooper here grows it himself. Captain Green-thumb, that's what people used to call him out on Panic tour." He turned to Cooper and smiled, added, "You out-done yourself this time, Coop. Y'all think we could puff a little while we wait?"

"What the fuck is a Panic tour?" Troy said, ignoring Sancho's request.

"Widespread Panic. It's a band," Cooper said in a flat voice.

"Ain't no goddamn band I ever heard of," Troy replied.

"You got something to play some tunes?" Sancho asked. "I can hook some up off my iPod. Hell, you'll probably love it, best music on earth, right, Davis?"

Davis nodded but didn't say a word.

"What the fuck is wrong with this one?" Troy asked, gesturing with his hand at Davis, his eyes vacant of anything resembling emotion.

"He's just quiet," Cooper said. "Unlike some of us."

Bobby figured that made Davis the smartest one out of all of them in that moment. If he could, he'd tie a fucking muzzle around Sancho's face, keep his stupid ass safe for the next half-hour until they could get through this fiasco. He didn't want anyone to get killed, at least.

CHAPTER THIRTY-SIX

Kirkpatrick and Perez had Meadows drop them off from Kirkpatrick's truck a quarter mile down the road from Troy Burnell's ranch, both wearing camouflage ponchos that Meadows had picked up for them over at Gander Mountain. She hadn't been happy about being left out of the action, and had let him know. Kirkpatrick felt bad, knowing she'd probably been treated to a host of being left out during her relatively short career in law enforcement. Still, he needed someone on the ground with a vehicle to come in and provide backup once the arrest was made. *If* the arrest was made.

He didn't like the looks of this situation, so far. Having to hike out through the pine trees and sandy-loam dry creek beds onto Troy Burnell's property, possibly breaking a host of rules in the process, but not having much choice.

The plan was for Meadows to signal them by radio once the deal was done, then Kirkpatrick and Perez would waltz in and put everyone under the muzzle, take them into custody with the help of some backup from the state troopers in the area, if need be. It was by far the sloppiest setup he could ever remember being a part of, but nothing could be done to help it.

They moved through the trees, trying to keep an eye out for anyone lurking around, the pine needles padding their steps and covering their tracks pretty well, actually. The problem they encountered once they got closer to Troy Burnell's barn was that it sat in the middle of a big, open field, meaning they would have to cover maybe a hundred yards on foot once it was time to move in and break up the deal. Kirkpatrick didn't like the looks of that, said so to Perez.

"Least there's not any sniper fire to worry about," Perez said.

"That we know of," Kirkpatrick corrected. He scanned the property, but couldn't see anyone on the roof or in the windows of the two-story, red-brick house adjacent to the barn. But that didn't mean there wasn't anyone there. He'd like to think that Troy Burnell was pretty comfortable dealing with these two amateurs and wouldn't bother with any major security, but the man's family hadn't gotten where they were by not being careful. All violent stories about Troy aside. Meadows had filled him in on Burnell's file, and he sounded like a real sociopath, though not necessarily the sharpest knife in the drawer, once he got angry. What he lacked in intelligence he seemed to make up for in brutality, and one thing experience had taught Kirkpatrick was that brutality went a long way toward filling in the gaps.

They were just settling in beneath some rough underbrush when Meadows came in on the radio, the concern obvious in her voice.

"Y'all copy?" she asked.

Kirkpatrick took the radio out from under his parka, noting it was covered in condensation from the sweat draining out of every pore in his body.

"I copy. What's up, over?" Kirkpatrick said in a dampened voice.

"Got some bad news. Just drove by a sheriff's cruiser parked about a quarter mile from the target's entrance, and wouldn't you know it, inside was Desmond Charles. Guy is Jack Gables' biggest lackey by far. That means Gables is tangled up in this mess almost for certain. Over."

Kirkpatrick and Perez made eye contact. Perez looked a little spooked maybe, but ready for action, making Kirkpatrick again glad he'd decided to get him the special detail for this case. He trusted Perez, guy was as standup as they came. He didn't want to get him into a situation where he might get hurt, though.

"Maybe he's just racking up numbers on traffic stops, over," Kirkpatrick said, not believing it for a second.

"I doubt it. Des doesn't work that kind of junk. You want my opinion, he's planning on making one specific traffic stop, and our boys are the target."

"You think they're working the old school roshambo?" Perez asked Kirkpatrick. "Make the deal legit, let their crooked cop friends lift the cash off them on the way out of town, no one the wiser?"

"Maybe," Kirkpatrick said. "We get our way, they won't make it that far."

"You guys want me to try and keep eyes on him, over?" Meadows asked.

Kirkpatrick's response was halted by the sound of a shotgun racking just behind his head. "Drop the radio if y'all wanna keep breathing," the voice that accompanied it said.

Kirkpatrick set the radio on the soft ground in front of him, eased his hands up near his head. "Y'all can come up off them pistols stashed up in your back waistbands, too," the voice added. "Nice and easy, ain't no way I'm gonna miss from two feet away. You boys move through the woods like a couple lost kids looking to get rescued. Now drop."

Kirkpatrick reached back and eased his Ruger SR40c to

the ground, saw Perez do the same. It was funny the way they had the same taste in weapons. Even funnier to have that thought while staring down the barrel of a shotgun. Perez's face was stoic, like this wasn't the first time someone had pointed a shotgun at him. As to whether it would be the last, they'd just have to see.

"Now crawl on y'all's knees over to that tree over there, sit with your back's against it, legs out straight in front of you. Keep your hands in contact with the ground the whole way or I will fucking blast you both to pieces."

They crawled on hands and knees to the base of a large Ponderosa pine and sat on their butts up against it. The man, large with a thick beard and dressed head to toe in Ducks Unlimited camouflage gear and pants tucked into what looked to be Gortex combat boots, reached down and picked up the radio Kirkpatrick had been using. He looked confused as he noticed the Teller County Sheriff's label stuck to the side, said, "Y'all working with Jack?" almost to himself.

"Of course we are," Perez said, "Now quit pointing that duck gun at us, will you?" The man met Perez's eyes and studied them for a moment, then smiled. "You must think we a bunch of country-ass bumpkins, huh? Tell you what. Y'all roll over onto your stomachs and stretch your arms out above your heads like you diving. Let's have a look at your wallets."

Having no choice, Kirkpatrick and Perez again complied, Kirkpatrick glad they weren't out in the pasture to end up face down in a pile of shit from one of the Longhorns grazing in it. The ground smelled like pine needles and musky rot. Kirkpatrick felt electricity pump through his body as the man reached for his wallet, his instinct to fight almost taking over his better sense. Almost. He hoped Perez wouldn't do anything stupid, but knew him to be pretty level-headed, so he doubted it. There wasn't much to do, anyway.

The man took in a deep chest full of air when he opened Kirkpatrick's wallet. Kirkpatrick's Ranger's badge was probably the last thing he expected to see inside it. When the radio pumped to life with Meadow's voice saying, "You want me to keep eyes on him, over?" the big man startled so much he would have shot them if his finger had been inside the trigger guard. He raised his boot high and stomped the radio flat, as if he were smashing a Coke can. Kirkpatrick flinched as pieces of the plastic flew past his face.

"Ain't this some shit," the man said to himself. He checked Perez's wallet, too, but it had no badge, Perez apparently having left his Travis County credentials back in Austin. "All right, boys, here's the skinny. You, the Mexican one," he said, pointing the shotgun's barrel at Perez, "reach onto this one here's belt and get his cuffs out, cuff him behind his back."

"Hell no," Perez said, like he meant it. The big man moved fast as he stepped forward and kicked Perez in the side of the head, his foot making a distinct thump that made it clear he'd kicked him hard. Perez's head slumped to the dirt and Kirkpatrick couldn't tell if he was still conscious, was a little surprised when Perez said, "All right, give me a minute," and eased up onto his knees, shaking off what must have been major cobwebs from the blow. His face was already starting to swell, Kirkpatrick could see that from the corner of his eye. As Perez slipped the cuffs on, Kirkpatrick had the distinct feeling that they were pretty well fucked.

After the man had taken Perez's cuffs and cuffed him, too, he stood them up by the chains, same as a lawman would do. "Let's get you boys inside and see what Troy wants to do with y'all," the man said. As they walked across the pasture with him pointing the shotgun at their backs, Kirkpatrick was already dreading the look on Daniels's and Davis's faces when they realized how much more trouble they were suddenly mired in.

CHAPTER THIRTY-SEVEN

Cooper's heart almost bounced right out of his chest when the ranger and his partner came walking through the door in cuffs, a big redneck motherfucker behind them with a shotgun pointed at their backs. He almost considered making a break for the door, but looked over at Davis and realized his best friend was frozen in space at the sight. No way he was leaving Davis behind. Besides, they probably wouldn't make it across the room before someone spread the backs of their heads across the floor.

"Who the fuck is this?" Troy said.

"Found these two in the woods across yonder. This one's got a Texas Ranger's badge in his wallet, the other one had a Teller County Sheriff's radio, said he works for Jack. They was talking to some female on the radio, too, her going on about Des sitting out on the roadside."

Sancho's head perked up at the word "sheriff's" and he made eye contact with Cooper, who shrugged, not knowing what else to do. Troy bowed his chest up and snarled.

"So you brought them here. Have you lost your country-ass mind? Texas Ranger, huh?" he snapped, looking ready to wreck someone, Cooper thinking it could literally be anyone in the room, hard to tell. "I can guarantee you whoever the fuck they are," Troy continued, "they ain't with Jack. Which makes me wonder how they got here." Troy glared at Sancho, who still looked confused, if

217

not completely sketched out.

"Why you looking at me, man? Cops freak me the fuck out," Sancho said. He turned to Bobby, who seemed to be brooding so hard that he hadn't noticed this new development. "Bobby, tell him what's up. I avoid pigs like an Islamic extremist."

Bobby shook his head and eyed Troy like a man whose car had stalled out on the train tracks. "I have no idea what the fuck is going on, Uncle Troy. But I don't think Sancho would sell us out."

Troy waved his hand at the man with the shotgun, said, "Merle, put those two out in the RV garage, tie them to something, whatever you gotta do. I'll be out there in a minute to get some answers. I need to discuss this with Jack first."

Merle complied, took the two cops out the side door while Cooper and Davis exchanged looks from the couch as if it were a ship that was sinking. Troy took out a burner phone and dialed a number.

"Yeah, it's me," he said into it. "We got a problem. You send a couple guys out here, one of 'em a Texas Ranger?" Troy paused as a voice said something through the speaker. "That's what I figured. Well, I got two of 'em tied up out in the RV shed, and they got some lady with eyes on Des out on the road, too. And she was carrying one of your department's radios. How you want me to proceed?" Troy paused while the voice on the other end shouted something Cooper couldn't make out, though he could tell the person, who must be Jack, was fucking furious. "Of course I called you, why the fuck not? You supposed to be my cover from this kind of bullshit. Just have Des grab the girl, she's gotta be nearby to him."

The voice shouted something else and went silent. Troy took the phone away from his face and looked at the screen.

It must have been dead because he tossed it onto the bar and went around the back of it, came out with a chrome-plated .45 and pointed it at Sancho's chest. "Take off your shirt, you curly-headed motherfucker. Don't make me say it twice. In fact, strip down naked."

Davis let out a whimper at that, the wire strapped to him probably feeling like an anchor pulling him under, now. Sancho's eyes narrowed and Cooper knew right away what was coming. Guy never knew when to keep his mouth shut.

"Just take it easy, Uncle Troy," Bobby said, looking the appropriate level of alarmed now. "We can figure all this out."

Troy turned and pointed the pistol at Bobby for a second. "You just shut your fucking mouth, you little shit. Mr. Bigshot, college man. You ain't never been nothing but a fuck-up. Even your daddy knew it. He was here right now he'd be pulling the skin off his face in shame at what kind of son he raised. Now sit down over there and don't so much as fucking breathe unless I tell you to." Troy turned back to Sancho, who still hadn't taken off his shirt.

"You gonna take off your clothes, boy, or you want me to take off your head instead?"

Sancho's face contorted. "What the fuck is this bullshit, Bobby? Thought you said it was all in the family, nothing to worry about? Now I got this big aggressive dude pointing a pistol at me? All I tried to do was hook you up with some—"

Sancho's face evaporated when Troy pulled the trigger, blood and bits of brain matter spraying the wall behind him. Cooper and Davis gasped in unison, too stunned from the pistol's report to do much else. Then all hell broke loose.

CHAPTER THIRTY-EIGHT

Kirkpatrick knew exactly what the quick look Perez gave him meant as the redneck with the scattergun led them into the room adjacent to the one where Burnell's guys were weighing out the weed. *Soon as that door closes, it's kill or be killed.* He felt bad for Cooper Daniels and Trevor Davis, but not much he could do for them in this moment, not unless he and Perez got free. It would be two on one, but they were cuffed, so not really. The shotgun was one hell of an equalizer either way. There was no way Troy Burnell could let them live after what they'd seen, and everything Meadows had told him regarding Burnell said they were on their way to the gallows. It was time to fight. The guy might get one of them, but maybe not both, and chances were they would both be dead either way if they didn't take this one last chance to fight.

"Y'all know we got backup on the way, right?" Perez said to the redneck, whose name was apparently Merle.

"No, you don't," Merle said in a flat, disinterested tone. "My guess is you got your girlfriend or some skanch wannabe chick cop sitting out on the road, but Des will take care of her. You had backup you wouldn't be using a Teller County radio, guaranteed."

Kirkpatrick had to give the guy credit for figuring that. He was working to think up a distraction when a shot popped off in the room behind them.

"There's our backup now," Kirkpatrick bluffed. Merle froze, swung the shotgun barrel toward the door behind them as he shifted to look. In unison Perez hit him in the knees while Kirkpatrick slipped his shoulder inside the barrel's trajectory and slammed into Merle's torso. The man was so stout that they damn near bounced off, but with Perez wrapping his body around Merle's legs Kirkpatrick was able to stay close enough to slam his forehead into Merle's chin.

It was enough to knock him off balance and send him crashing to the floor, his finger pulling the trigger and firing a shot off into space as he landed. The report dazed Kirkpatrick, but he kept fighting anyway. Perez clung to Merle's legs using the bend in his torso as Kirkpatrick drove his forehead into Merle's face again, then again, and managed to use his foot to kick the shotgun out of reach.

"You boys is dead when I get up," Merle gurgled through a bloody mouth.

"Who says you're getting up?" Kirkpatrick said as he dropped another big head butt and felt the man weaken a bit. He hit him with another one, this time to the nose, and was seeing stars then. Blood shot up like a geyser from Merle's face as Perez rolled off his legs and managed to stand up. Perez stomped on Merle's head so hard Kirkpatrick thought it might kill him. It took two more good stomps to finally render him unconscious.

"Jesus fucking Christ," Kirkpatrick said as he rolled off Merle and used the wall to stand himself up. "That was one country-fed son of a bitch."

"Sure was. Now get over here and see if you can't manage my handcuff keys out of my pocket, the dumb motherfucker didn't even bother to take them."

It took them some trouble, looking like a couple of amputees playing Twister, but finally Kirkpatrick managed to get the keys out. It took another thirty seconds to figure out how to get them in the hole with them standing back to back. Soon as Perez was free he returned the favor.

Perez busied himself searching for their weapons in Merle's shell bag. It was almost like he'd actually been out hunting, not guarding the perimeter of a drug deal. More shots popped off in the room behind them as Perez found the weapons.

"Well, shall we?" Kirkpatrick said, gripping his Ruger, thinking nothing had ever felt so precious in his hands before.

CHAPTER THIRTY-NINE

Initially, Bobby was frozen in place once Troy pulled the trigger. But it was like he'd been thinking about this for weeks, and the idea had sunk in so deep that it had become the only possible option. It took him a second to get moving, but once he did, he just whipped out his pistol and fired blindly in Troy's direction, hitting him in the bicep of his gun hand, which caused him to drop the .45.

He turned the pistol and fired at George, but the big black son of a bitch had already turned over the table and ducked behind it. He knew it had been a mistake to shift his focus in that direction when Troy's full bodyweight hit him with a double-leg takedown, turned him upside down and dropped him flat on his head, making him see stars.

"You gonna shoot *me*, motherfucker?" Troy yelled as he slid his knees up under Bobby's armpits, using his bloody arm as if he hadn't even been shot. "So much for family."

As if Troy even cared. Of all the things Bobby could be thinking about in that moment the one thought he had was that he'd forgotten to switch his clip of target ammo out for hollow points, that the bullet must have gone right through Troy's arm without inflicting much damage. It was gonna take more than a hole in his arm to stop a psychopath like Troy. Troy slammed a left fist into Bobby's head, bouncing it off the concrete floor. After that Bobby was too woozy to really feel the barrage of shots that Troy rained down on him. Then, just as suddenly as they'd started, the punches stopped. Bobby rolled over onto his stomach, faintly aware that Troy was no longer on top of him, but also fading fast out of consciousness. He gasped for air and spit out a few teeth, unable to breathe through what must be a broken nose. The last thing he heard was the unmistakable popping of gunfire, then he dropped out of reality like freefalling from an airplane.

CHAPTER FORTY

When the shots started flying Cooper grabbed Davis by the forearm and dragged him to the floor, started army crawling toward the door without even thinking about it. As they crawled he worked up the courage to look up, where he saw that Bobby was getting his ass stomped by Troy in spite of having just shot him. The crawling was slow, Cooper trying to keep some sort of furniture between them and the action as much as he could, worrying like hell that one or both of them would catch a stray bullet.

Then the Ranger and his partner came back through the door, armed now and headed straight for Troy, who had gotten off Bobby and crawled over to where his pistol was laying against the wall.

Troy gripped it and stood up over Bobby, was just getting ready to execute him when Kirkpatrick said, "I wouldn't do it if you want to keep that shiny-ass haircut on top of your head."

Cooper ducked his head again and kept crawling, under the obnoxious pool table, then beyond it, Davis hot on his trail. He had no intention of staying to see how this played out. He could feel his truck keys digging into his pocket. If they could just get to the truck they could roll out of this nightmare and point it straight back to Colorado, hope to never hear another word about this thing again. Or if they did, admit to being afraid for their lives, claim to have gone into shock or something, hope it bought some mercy.

They were ten feet from the door and Cooper couldn't help but look back one more time. Mostly what he saw was Troy holding his hands up, the pistol hanging from the index finger of his left hand.

But he also saw something the Ranger and his partner couldn't see, which was the big, black country boy Troy had called George coming up from behind the table where Cooper's weed was strewn across the floor, a pistol of his own in hand. For a moment, Cooper considered just charging out the door, figured no one would pay any attention to them and they could be out of town before it mattered. If the guy killed the Ranger there was a chance no one would ever bother them about this again, and he could go straight, be a father, get the rest of his life together. Yeah, right.

Soon as the thought crossed his mind he knew that he couldn't do that; even if it would work, it just wouldn't be right. He looked back at Davis and pointed to the door, indicated for him to keep crawling. Then he was on his feet, moving stealthily across the room at first, then sprinting as George raised the pistol to fire. George noticed him coming right as he came into striking distance and the distraction was just enough that his shot popped off over the Ranger's head, then Cooper tackled George across the bow like his dad had taught him before he started playing middle school football.

The hit spun George around before he shrugged it off, clearly some sort of athlete or football player himself in the past. Right away, Cooper thought, I'm dead, a thought further confirmed when George swung the pistol toward him, backing away toward the door now to get some distance.

Just as George prepared to fire, something struck him

from behind and he crumpled, though he still got the shot off. The bullet's impact hit Cooper in the abdomen and he was sure it would be the last thing he ever felt. He dropped to the floor feeling as if someone had set his insides on fire, curled into the fetal position out of instinct, his hands on the spot where the bullet had entered. When he looked back up he saw Davis standing above an unconscious George, holding one of the gaudy pool balls in his hand, a terrified look on his face.

"Shit, Coop, you're hit!" he yelled. Cooper opened his eyes again to find himself facing the officers, who had taken their eyes off Troy Burnell during the commotion. Cooper tried to call out to them but Burnell was too fast, closed the distance and used his right arm to yank Perez's gun arm across his body, spinning him around. He had his arm around Perez's neck before the cop could even react to it. Somewhere in the motion he had come up with Perez's gun, too, which he held to Perez's head with his shaky, wounded arm.

Kirkpatrick panned him with his own gun. Cooper could feel his blood leaking out of his belly, started to get woozy, his vision blurring. Was this what it felt like to die?

"Drop it or he dies," Troy Burnell said to the ranger. "Two seconds and I shoot, make up your mind. One..."

Cooper could just make out the ranger's form as he held his own gun over his head, kneeled down and set it on the floor while saying, "All right, you got it, bud. Take it easy."

"Take it easy? Kick that thing over to me before I shoot your leg off. Take it easy... Man comes into my house to try and destroy my life and he tells me to—"

A pistol's pop cut off the rest of the sentence as Troy's head became little more than a red mist on Perez's face. His body slumped straight down to the floor so that his legs folded directly under him in an unnatural way, like a boxer who gets dropped right where he's standing. Cooper tried to turn his head to see who had shot, but all he could see was a blur of blonde hair somewhere near the front door, and even that faded off. He felt a strange coldness that seemed to be inside him rather than out. He could feel Davis touching him, but he seemed miles away, more like an apparition than a physical being occupying the same space and time. Part of him felt as if he'd taken too much LSD and been shot like a rocket right off the planet and between two stars. *What a way to die*, Cooper thought as darkness surrounded him. *Please don't let me die without seeing my child at least once.*

CHAPTER FORTY-ONE

The newscasters hadn't made it look pretty, that much was beyond clear to Kirkpatrick as he knocked back the boilermaker's sidecar of Buffalo Trace and washed it down with some microbrew the bartender told him paired well with it. He tapped his fingers on the tiled bar top and looked around the small airport lounge, but nobody seemed to be watching. It had been on the tips of everyone's tongues for the last two weeks straight, but now the twenty-four-hour news cycle had finally found another frank to skewer. This was the first mention he'd seen of it in a day or two, not that he'd been watching television anyway.

"Senator Weldon Robb again today denied the massive outcry for him to resign amid continued suggestion that he may have used his political influence to seek revenge on Austin resident Elroy Watts, who was killed two and a half weeks ago during a drug deal gone wrong that involved ex-Heisman Trophy winner and NFL burnout Bobby Burnell. Burnell is set to testify in front of a grand jury on Monday, but sources report he will likely invoke his Fifth Amendment right, further complicating an already murky and complex case.

"Both the Texas Rangers and the Teller County Sheriff's Department have released official statements denying that Ranger Russ Kirkpatrick and Travis County Deputy Javier Perez were working for a covert task force when the event occurred, a task force alleged to have been put together at Senator Robb's request to seek revenge on the man allegedly responsible for the tragic suicide death of Robb's nineteen-year-old grandson, Carson Robb, last year."

Kirkpatrick pushed back from the bar and leaned down to pick up his carry-on duffle, which he'd been using to travel since his days in the military years ago. He still didn't know if he was happy or angry to see fellow law enforcement agencies closing the ranks around him, considering it meant they were closing around Jack Gables in the process. At the end of the day, he and Perez had been left with nothing but a few mentions of Jack's first name on tape, and a pile of dead bodies to explain to the world.

Leave it to Weldon Robb to stand his ground when everyone on the planet knew it was time to retreat. At this point Kirkpatrick felt lucky his superiors had let him resign, though he knew they hadn't done it for him. They'd done it to cover up scandal. Chain of command had not only approved his special assignment to Robb's task force, they'd ordered it. Now here he was standing alone in an airport lounge, career in the shitter, but finally on his way to Mahahual at long last.

Not that he'd handled things very professionally. No backup, no real plan. He'd played this one by the seat of his pants and then been surprised when his ass caught on fire and burned up. It had been all he could do to fall on his sword and save Perez from losing his job, though as far as Kirkpatrick knew, his buddy would be writing two a.m. parking tickets for the rest of his natural life down on Sixth Street.

He walked out of the lounge and into the bathroom, dropped off the two whiskey drinks he'd had, and made his way to the gate. He still had an hour before the flight. Maybe Meadows would still show up. Probably not. Things had pretty damn well fallen apart between them, once it came time to start lying for their superiors. She hadn't wanted to do it. "We need to tell the truth," she kept saying when the bosses and higher-ups had insisted Kirkpatrick meet with her so he could talk sense into her.

They'd let him know in no uncertain terms whose ass would fry if the official story didn't become canon for everyone involved. Finally she'd relented, but only for the sake of saving his ass, of that much he was sure. She'd probably never forgive him for it, though that hadn't stopped him from emailing her tickets to come with him, just in case. Given that he'd pretty damn well ruined her career, too, he figured she could use the time off. She'd saved his ass in taking out Troy Burnell. Now he was having trouble saving hers, and that made him feel like shit. He had no idea where she was currently, figured he might not ever know again.

He sat in one of the black mid-century chairs that every single airport in the country seemed to have, wondering if that, too, was just another insider scam. He'd almost dozed off when the man across from him looked at the television above his head, then back at him, then up, then back at him again.

"Hey, you're the guy from the television," the old man said, almost a question, fingering himself in the ear out of confusion as he spoke.

"Not anymore," Kirkpatrick replied, then tipped his hat down over his eyes to show he was done discussing it. He wondered what his kids would say to him the next time he saw them, if he ever saw them again. That neither had called him when the story broke spoke volumes as to how they must feel about the whole thing. They were both probably more worried about how it would affect their own lives than they were about what would happen to their father.

Maybe he hadn't been as good a father as he should. He drifted off thinking about that, wondering what kind of redemption he might find for himself down the line. For now, the only thing he was interested in was sticking the biggest tarpon he could stick on the end of a fishing rod every day for the next month or two. That, and a couple of fresh pina coladas at Nacional Beach Club's quiet beachside bar. Hell, he might not ever come back to this nightmare again, if he could help it. At least a man could dream that. He had a feeling this whole shit storm would be sucking him back in soon enough.

Maybe Meadows would still show.

By his watch he had at least a half-hour before the flight began to board, and not much else left to lose.

CHAPTER FORTY-TWO

"Y'all just about done trimming up that Sour Diesel?" Cooper asked the ten trimmers sitting around the industrial metal table with rubber gloves and masks on.

"Won't be long, another pound or so," one of them, Carl, said.

"Come let me know when it's processed, let's move it all over to sweat in coolers for a day or two before we set it up for retail."

As he made his way back to the front end of the warehouse, he fingered the scar on his abdomen, just as he did almost once an hour, it seemed like. It had been four months now since he'd almost lost his life. He still couldn't believe the way things had worked out.

His cellphone rang, pulling him back out of the memories. He checked the screen, then swiped to answer it.

"Hey, Josie, you feeling better today?" he said.

"I'm feeling a little better," she replied. "Wanted to remind you we have the Lamaze classes tonight. You're still coming with me, right?"

"You bet. At seven, right?"

"Yes. Do you still have the address?"

Cooper swiped to his text list, confirmed it, and then said, "Sure do. You made any decisions about moving yet?" It might annoy her that he brought it up, but he couldn't help it. The thought of her going away and taking their unborn child with her tore him up inside.

"Cooper...I don't know. Like I told you, I'm still thinking it over. I don't want to fight about this right now, okay?"

"Who's fighting?" Cooper asked. "I'm at work, actually. Just, please, you gotta understand, baby. I've got a good job here now, and it's something I can't do down in Texas. Plus that place is dangerous for me now. But I don't want to live so far away from my child. You've got a good life here, too."

It seemed like no matter how legit he went something always came between him and his passion for cultivation. The difference was now he was a taxpaying member of society, the head grower at High Country Cannabis Cooperative, which had five locations now across the city. He was making good money, and finally in the position to really be the partner Josie needed. It was just that he'd gone too far, taking that last illegal crop to Texas and almost getting himself and Davis killed. Now she didn't trust him anymore, maybe never would.

"We can get some dinner after the class tonight and talk about this, Cooper, that's the best I can say. I care about you, but I have to make the decisions that are right for my life now, with or without you."

Cooper sighed. No use arguing with her. It wouldn't get him what he wanted, which was to have her back, be with his family. He forced himself to smile instead, hoped it would carry through the phone on his voice. "I understand where you're coming from, Jos, I really do. Just... thanks for letting me come along and be a part of this stuff, it means a lot to me."

"I'm glad you're getting your life together, Cooper. Really I am. I can't promise you any more than that. See you tonight."

"Sounds good," Cooper said, but she was already off

the line. The phone rang again before he could even put it back in his pocket. Davis.

"Hey, brother, what's up?" Cooper said by way of answering the call.

"Not much, man, how's work?"

"Good. Great crop of Sour Diesel just turned out, bosses are ecstatic with the quality of the product under my soil recipe and feeding regimen."

"They'd have to be crazy to feel any other way. So listen, Candace and I are smoking a brisket, been at it all day, wanted to see if you could come over tonight for dinner and check out the new place?"

"I'd love to, brother. But I've got Lamaze classes with Josie at seven. Maybe I can stop by afterward, if it doesn't run too long? We're supposed to go out to dinner and talk things over after, but that probably won't happen."

"Well shit, man, that's great. I hope you work it out. We can just catch up tomorrow, no big deal. You going to Government Mule on Friday? Looks like we've got a pretty big crew together."

"Nah, I'm gonna get caught up on work up here. Growing at this scale is crazy enough as it is, but when you add in the paperwork that it takes to track it all for the government, it's almost never-ending. Next time?"

"Next time it is. Holler at me."

"Will do," Cooper said, then hung up. He went to his office, barely more than a closet tucked off the back corner of the twenty-thousand-square-foot grow warehouse, which was pumping a good five hundred thousand watts of high pressure sodium lamps, growing more than fifty strains beneath their orange shine. He looked out over that sea of cannabis and couldn't help but smile. This really was his dream job. With the company stock options they'd offered him, it would mean long-term stability if he could do it well.

His mind drifted back again to the night he'd gotten shot. It had changed everything, lying there believing he was dying that way. He'd saved Ranger Kirkpatrick's life, and the man had done him the ultimate favor and left him and Davis out of the meat of his report, hung the weed and everything else on Sancho, who was way too dead to care.

Cooper shuddered as he remembered the look on Sancho's face right before Troy Burnell murdered him. Sanch had been a maniac, but he'd still been a friend, and he'd miss some of the wild times they'd had together, although most wild times in general were behind him now.

There was a good chance he'd get called in front of the grand jury that was set up to decide whether to arraign any and all of them on various charges, ranging from trafficking to murder, but so long as they all stuck to the plan, things would be okay. That had been the craziest part, standing there with three cops and a former Heisman Trophy winner, coming up with a story that would hopefully keep them all out of the pen. Putting everything on Troy and Sancho had been the best fit for all involved.

The FBI wanted Bobby to testify against Jack Gables, otherwise they had nothing on him. But Bobby wasn't talking to them, no doubt had a deal of his own worked out with Gables that involved him keeping his life for closing his mouth. His uncle Troy's lone henchman, a lifelong criminal and probably a crony of that crooked sheriff Jack Gables, too, had simply disappeared without a trace.

"Cooper?" It was Carl, his mask pulled up on top of his head now.

"Yeah, man, what's up?"

"Sour D's all finished up. You want us to start on the Flo now?"

"Yeah, let's pull just the driest ones down and trim them up, we don't need to get through the whole batch today,

236

they're not all dry enough to process yet anyway."

"Ten-four," Carl said. "I'll let you know how far we get."

Cooper nodded and Carl made his way off to get back to work.

Cooper looked out over that sea of green plants again, watched as his workers made their way up the rows, watering plants, trimming the branches off that were too low to get enough light for viable buds, spraying neem oil on the sections with plants more prone to pests. That was the hardest part of growing at this scale: it made it nearly impossible to get rid of all the pests. Lately, his own life felt that way.

If he was lucky, he could keep the pests from his own past at bay and finally move into the life he'd been dreaming about since he was a kid. It might not be too much to ask, just needed a little luck and a lot of faith in his friends. All he could do for now was hold on tight and try to enjoy the ride.

ACKNOWLEDGMENTS

Big shout out to all my friends and family, especially those I've lost touch with over the years. Please holler at me! Thank you to my mom, Kathy Mitchell, your support has meant everything to me. George Mitchell, you know you're one of my favorite people, right? For my new wife Stephanie, a true phoenix rising from the ashes to fly. Keaton and Tucker, don't grow up too fast boys. Nathan and Heidi Beauchamp, y'all will never know how much you did for me, I owe you my life. Chris Barili and the rest of the Master Assassins, y'all are the best. Steve Fulton—thank you for everything, you're the best beast in the west. Thank you Michaela Roessner for first telling me I was a crime writer—that changed everything. Russell Davis and Mark Todd, thanks for the lessons. Tim and Becky Harris, thanks for taking me into the family with open arms. Ralph Martin, you're always in my heart, smartest man I ever met. Eric Campbell, THANK YOU for investing in my work, it means the world to me. To any magazine who has ever published one of my stories, y'all are the unsung heroes of the writing world, so thank you. Last but not least: everyone who has ever bothered to read anything I ever wrote. Even if you hated it, my sincere thanks. There's so much more to come, so strap up your boots.

Michael Pool was born and raised in Tyler, Texas and educated on the Western Slope of Colorado, where he lived for nearly twenty years. He has worked as a private investigator, Brazilian Jiu-Jitsu instructor, bellhop, used car salesman (the worst ever), content marketing copywriter, and in other more nefarious positions better left unnamed. His other books include the crime noir novella *Debt Crusher* and a collection of short stories, *New Alleys for Nothing Men*. *Texas Two-Step* is his first full-length novel, and will be followed up by *Rose City* in 2019. His short stories have appeared in numerous magazines, journals, and anthologies. He lives in Dallas with his wife Stephanie, stepsons Keaton and Tucker, and ferocious little lions London and Walter-Kitty.

MichaelPool.net

BOOKS

On the following pages are a few
more great titles from the
Down & Out Books publishing family.

For a complete list of books and to
sign up for our newsletter,
go to DownAndOutBooks.com.

Tushhog
A Scotland Ross Novel
Jeffery Hess

Down & Out Books
May 2018
978-1-946502-60-5

It's 1981 in Fort Myers, Florida, where Scotland Ross squares off with a redneck clan, a Cuban gang, a connected crew from New York, and one friend who does him wrong.

Crimes of violence, drugs, and theft pale in comparison to the failure of self-restraint.

Tushhog is a story of compulsion, the types of people who take what isn't theirs, and the repercussions that follow.

Abnormal Man
Grant Jerkins

ABC Group Documentation,
an imprint of Down & Out Books
978-1-943402-39-7

Chaos? Or fate? What brought you here? Were the choices yours, or did something outside of you conspire to bring you to this place? Because out in the woods, in a box buried in the ground, there is a little girl who has no hope of seeing the moon tonight. The moon has forsaken her. Because of you.

Dead Guy in the Bathtub
Stories by Paul Greenberg

All Due Respect, an imprint of
Down & Out Books
March 2018
978-1-946502-87-2

Crime stories with a dark sense of humor and irony. These characters are on the edge and spiraling out of control. Bad situations become serious circumstances that double down on worst-case scenarios. A Lou Reed fan gets himself caught on the wild side. A couple goes on a short and deadly crime spree. A collector of debts collecting a little too much for himself. A vintage Elvis collection to lose your head over. A local high school legend with a well-endowed reputation comes home.

This debut collection is nothing but quick shots of crime fiction.

The Place of Refuge
Albert Tucher

Shotgun Honey, an imprint of
Down & Out Books
978-1-943402-61-8

Detective Errol Coutinho of the Hawaii County Police has a serial killer of prostitutes to catch and a shortage of leads to pursue. Office Jessie Hokoana of the Honolulu P.D. has an undercover assignment that tests her loyalties and takes her to the brink of death.

When their cases collide in the rainforest of the Big Island, family ties turn deadly, and there may be no *pu'uhonua*—no place of refuge—for anyone.